Passion's Revenge

Sometimes the Price of Love is Deadly

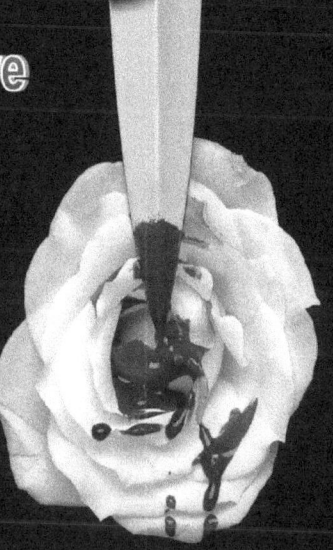

By Jai Colvin

Table of Contents

JAI CALVIN

Passion's Revenge

Re.ad Publishing, Inc.

PASSION'S REVENGE

Published in the United States by Re.ad Publishing/July, 2015
First published by the author in 2002.

Re.ad Publishing, Inc.
145 Corte Madera Town Center, Suite 437
Corte Madera, CA 94925
Visit our website at www.readpublishing.com

Acquisitions Editor: Amanda Barnett

ISBN 978-1-63160-104-0, print
ISBN 978-1-63160-496-6, ebook

For TyAnne Colvin, without you there would be no Johni Andrews.

Chapter 1

The very first time she saw her she was caught off guard. Johni Andrews had always prided herself in never letting another woman attract her attentions so much that she lost her reasoning. Once in a lifetime had been enough. After the ordeal with Brenda, losing her mind over a woman was the last thing she was going to let happen again. A person can stand to have their heart ripped out and handed back to them only once before they realize that catching that bus again was a bad idea. Yet here she was standing in a crowded room at a party she had not planned to attend, trying to catch her breath.

The party, given by a couple Johni had done her best to avoid over the past couple of months, had been a bore until now. She'd all but given up and decided to go home when the most beautiful woman she'd ever seen walked through the door.

At first Johni thought she might be seeing things but like a vision from heaven itself the woman glided into the room and it had actually taken more than a few seconds before Johni started breathing again. She watched this incredibly graceful creature make her way around the room seemingly greeting everyone. Her skin was a deep olive although in her face it was difficult to place her in a specific heritage. Her hair was a golden brown with red highlights. Johni watched her as she worked the room in a shy but pleasant way, smiling at each person she greeted. She had the most incredible smile. "I have to meet her", Johni thought to herself, unconsciously she was now staring.

The woman made her way through the crowd nodding but something in her eyes told a different story. She was polite and gracious but her eyes conveyed a mild discomfort at all the attention. Johni started for the door once more, nope, she thought, nope ain't gonna happen. Intrigued as she was Johni turned to find one of women who had invited her to say good-bye and get the hell out before she did something she would regret. Turning she felt a chill run down her spine than right back up again as she found herself face to face with the very woman she had just been watching and had subsequently decided to run from. Johni was at a loss for words. Her head screamed, say something, anything, but her mouth would not move, instead she stood there looking into the eyes of this beautiful creature, and uttered not a sound.

"Hi." The woman said in tender voice the like of which Johni had never heard. Johni cleared her throat and nodded slightly.

"Hello". It was the only word Johni could find in the maze that was her mind. She was mesmerized. Someone nudged her from behind and Johni came out of her daze of fumbling for what to say next. Ricki, one of the two women giving the party stood by her side, a blessing and a curse all at the same time.

"This is our writer friend," Ricki was saying, "Johni Andrews. Johni, this is Raven Michaels," John offered her hand and Raven took it. Her touch was soft but deliberate.

"Nice to meet you," Was she crazy or did she just hear her voice go an octave lower than normal? Geez Johni, she admonished herself.

"A writer, what do you write?" Raven asked with a smile. Johni really had to control the urge to touch her again. She searched her mind madly for a proper way to answer the woman's question but finally resigned herself to the only real answer.

"Horror," Johni said suddenly wishing that she wrote romance novels.

"Scary stuff huh? How intriguing. Are you published?" No holding back, she was asking questions straight from the hip. Johni liked that.

"Yes, yes I am." Thank God, Johni thought to herself; be a really bad time to be a hack.

"Yes? Just yes?" Ricki threw her hands up in the air in mock exasperation, "Johni is a premiere writer. She has several books out on the shelf now, one on the best seller list." Johni look embarrassed but Raven looked impressed. She usually didn't like hearing her work run up the flag pole like that but for some reason tonight she was glad to have Ricki touting her work.

"Really? Maybe I'll have to read one. I've never known a famous writer before." Raven smiled and Johni felt the urge to ask her out right here in front of all these people. She looked down and cleared her throat again about to throw herself back into the dating fire when the woman was gone as suddenly as she had appeared. It wasn't until Raven was some ways across the room that Johni realized that she hadn't been taking full breaths. She was staring after her when with a poke in the ribs Ricki made it acutely clear that not only was she still there but she had also noticed Johni's interest. Oh good Christ, Johni thought, this is all I need.

"Take it you liked what you saw," Ricki asked. It was like suddenly finding yourself up to your elbows in nuclear fall-out, a real oh shit moment. Ricki was not exactly on Johni's top ten people-you-can-trust list. She talked, usually about everyone else's business and to everyone else in the room whether they knew you or not. Ricki was that childhood friend that you have and you put up with because, well, you've been friends since kindergarten, forever linked by school naps and a shared love of eating glue before you knew better. She couldn't help herself however she had to ask questions.

"Who was that?"

"Raven Michaels." Ricki said as if Johni should know exactly who she was. Frustrated she asked her question again.

"Who is Raven Michaels, Ricki?" Ricki smiled, Johni knew she enjoyed torturing people when she knew she had something they wanted. She was a gossipy woman and making people squirm was what she lived for. It was one of the reasons Johni avoided her so much on a normal basis. Ricki was one of those people whom she was friends with but if someone held a gun to her head Johni wouldn't be able to come up with a reason why except that whole kindergarten connection.

"Raven is from San Gabriel," Ricki offered. "She is one of the area's top medical researchers, you know, looking for cures and all of that type of thing. She has quite a reputation. I'm surprised you haven't heard of her. She made the local top 100 people to know last year." This was all fine and well but Johni still wasn't getting the answers she needed. She decided to just blurt out her real question before Ricki really launched into Raven's bio.

"Is she with anyone?"

"You mean does she have a girlfriend," Ricki teased. Johni hated this. If she'd wanted to dance she'd have asked someone. "Well?"

"Yes." Ricki answered. Johni's heart fell. Damn, she thought, wouldn't you know it, when you're straight all the good ones are married or gay and when you're gay the good ones are all straight or married, funny how that works. "You know though, I've heard that they aren't doing so well." Ricki was fishing and Johni didn't feel like going there. She was not the kind of person who dated women who were spoken for. It was disrespectful and just plain wrong. She searched the room and found Raven once again. She was holding what seemed a polite conversation with Maggie Bower, one of the local council people, next to the bar. Johni felt a slight tug at her heart but shook it off. If Raven Michaels had a girlfriend she was off limits

"That's too bad," Johni offered tearing her attention away from the woman across the room and focusing on Ricki. "Well, got to go Ricki, thanks for inviting me."

"What so soon? The party is just getting started. I had some other people I wanted you to meet," Ricki protested. That's what Johni was afraid of. It never fails that when you're single all of your coupled friends try to set you up. She had known this was the reason she'd been invited here tonight in the first place. On the one hand she was flattered that her friends thought so well of her but on the other hand it irritated her. As far as she was concerned tonight was already a bust anyway, the only woman worth talking to as far as she could see was otherwise occupied. Ricki made a few more futile attempts to make her stay but then finally gave in and said good-bye. Johni made her way towards the front door saying her good-byes. As she turned to leave, Raven caught her eye once again. She couldn't help but admire the woman. She was beautiful. She had to be about was about 5'2. She looked Italian with a beautiful light brown skin tone that made her smile somehow seem brighter. And what a smile it was, brighten the whole room yet there was sexy slyness to it as well. There was an air of intelligence about her with an underlying vulnerability. Class was a word brought to mind as well as warm and sensual. She wore elegance and grace like a parka. Johni couldn't help but stare a moment longer before leaving and to her amazement Raven turned towards her and their eyes met, she'd been caught. Raven's smile confirmed her suspicions. Slightly embarrassed but determined to hold her ground, Johni continued her gaze and to her delight Raven held hers as well for a few moments. Time appeared to have stopped and it felt as though they were the only two people in the room but just as Johni convinced herself to maybe stay after all and to take a step towards Raven another woman appeared at Raven's side. Johni didn't recognize her but she was a tall woman with short brown hair. She smiled while she spoke to Raven and Raven smiled back although she glanced once or twice back at Johni. This must be the not-doing-so-well girlfriend. Johni got her conformation seconds later when the new arrival leaned down and kissed Raven on the cheek. The new comer was pretty enough but somehow looked awkward next to Raven. Johni scorned herself for her thoughts, seeing what she wanted to see for sure. She was just interested in Ms. Michaels so she was subconsciously trying to make things bad between the woman and her girlfriend.

"Pathetic," Johni said to herself and she turned to leave. She put her hand on the doorknob and couldn't resist the urge to take one more look back at Raven she waited a few seconds until she caught her attention and nodded once more before leaving the party. As she stepped out onto the porch Johni pulled up her collar and tried to read the final look she thought she had seen in Raven's face. Was it disappointment?

* * *

Raven watched as Johni left. She felt a little disappointed for reasons that she couldn't seem to put her finger on. There weren't many times when she noticed people that left her longing for more. The woman hadn't been anything extraordinary. She was masculine but with an obvious soft edge. Raven liked that. She hadn't seemed to have much to say, strange for a writer. You would think that all a writer would do is talk. There had been something about the woman however that definitely caught her interest. She had a quiet assuredness that Raven had enjoyed while she stood there with her. It interested her. She had interested her. She felt the urge suddenly to know more. Turning to go find Ricki, Raven stopped as she felt a slight tug on her sleeve.

"Where are you going?" Andi asked looking suspicious. Raven wasn't in the mood to do this tonight. She knew that given the chance Andi would make this evening very difficult, it was just something she seemed to enjoy. Raven had never given her a reason to be jealous but it seemed as though Andi always found a reason anyway and what she didn't find she simply made up to suit her needs, there didn't even have to be another woman involved. Raven resigned herself to the task of coddling Andi and decided to let her investigation of Johni Andrews go for now. This would appear to be yet another outing tending to Andi's ego. She forced a smile.

"Nowhere really. I'd really like something to drink though." Andi looked perplexed but searched the room until she spotted the bar.

"What do you want? I could really use a beer." Andi said brightening it seemed at the thought of alcohol.

"Soda's fine."

"Okay, I'll be right back." Andi strolled off to the bar. Raven returned to her thoughts of Johni and her attentions to locating Ricki. Maybe she could ask just a few questions. It seemed that she'd just found Ricki when Andi reappeared back at her side with a glass of soda.

"Here you are." Andi handed Raven the glass. "Just the way you like it."

"Where are the cherries?" Raven asked playing with the straw in her glass.

"The what?"

"Nothing, never mind," she said quietly. Raven stood sipping her soda thinking about how after four years it still never occurred to Andi that she enjoyed cherries in her sodas. She ordered them every single time. Funny, she thought sarcastically, how some things never change. She watched Andi as she drank her beer. Raven cared about Andi but she felt no love any longer. Andi had grown into a chore, something she had to contend with because she had made a commitment. It was like wearing a pair of expensive shoes that you discovered hurt your feet after the initial purchase. Even though they hurt, you'd wear them anyway because you had spent so much money on them. Andi was immature and selfish. Some days it was like having a young child in the house. She had to smooth her ego and feed her self-esteem every day, and emotionally; Andi was a spoiled child who needed watching every minute. She had always tried to do what made Andi happy and she had always thought that if she just found the right button to push or the right needs to be met, maybe Andi would change. Andi however, also seemed to stay on top of what made Andi happy first. Not knowing Raven's habits after all this time was one of the ways Andi shined in the selfish department. She simply never paid attention. How could she after spending so much time and energy on herself? Hell she'd be willing to bet that Andi didn't even know her favorite color, despite all the blues and purples woven into their home.

"Come on Raven, let's dance," Andi said grabbing her hand. Raven sighed and let herself be led to the dance floor. Smiling to hide her disappointment she braced herself for another long night.

Chapter 2

This was not working. Johni never had this much trouble writing early in the morning. Over the years it had become her preference to get up first thing and write until she got tired or drained all the words out of her veins, whichever came first. Late afternoon found her too lazy and evenings were reserved for reading. Pushing back from her desk she went to the front window. She loved having a big picture window looking out into the world even though her friends had implied that it made the place seem too exposed. Perverts could look in, they had argued, but she loved it and the freedom it represented.

It was slightly over cast outside and the chill in the air was noticeable but not so much that you'd need anything more than a sweater. It was perfect writing weather. So what was the problem? She had been trying for two hours now and nothing. Her mind had done some serious wandering this morning. She thought about the party last night, and the fact that the jeep needed an oil change. She considered the people she'd seen at Ricki's and decided to wait until after lunch to do the dishes. She thought about Raven Michaels and her girlfriend and then noticed that the windows needed to be cleaned. Everything went through her mind but writing this damn story. Finally, giving in to the fact that she was not accomplishing anything this morning she decided to go out for brunch. Maybe that would clear her mind; food had that effect on her. Of course this was probably why she couldn't lose that extra ten pounds either. Ten minutes and she was pulling into Mac's.

Mac's was the one place of refuge Johni had in town. She enjoyed the solitude of living on the outskirts but when she needed a good meal and decent company she went to Mac's. Isaac Maclin was one of the nicest men Johni had ever met. The burly six foot two man was a hell of a cook and over the years had become a very good friend. He minded his own business and he never prodded her for answers the way her female friends did. Over time they had reached a sort of male bonding point in their relationship. There was trust between them and she had spent more than a few good times with Mac and his wife, Olie. She didn't share the same type of relationship with Olie but then was always trying to set Johni up with some woman. More than a few times she'd offended some poor heterosexual woman who had no clue that the well-meaning but noisy woman was just trying to fix up her lesbian friend. Normally this would have bugged the hell out of her but it was endearing coming from Olie. The three of them had more than a few laughs behind Olie's botched match making. Johni pushed through the front door and smiled, it felt like home and this morning both Mac and Olie were working.

Johni admired Mac and Olie's relationship. They were close and it showed. They had the kind of relationship most other people wanted, romantic yet a partnership in all aspects. As soon as they saw her the smiles on their faces said it all, she was part of the family.

"Well look who decided to grace us with her presence this morn," Olie said. Skipping around the end of the counter she hugged Johni in a way that only Olie could. She didn't just hug a person but folded them up into her arms as though she was a warm mothering blanket. It had taken Johni some time to get use to Olie's affectionate personality but once she did she enjoyed it. Johni always felt protected here. Hugging Olie back just as hard she winked at Mac over Olie's shoulder.

"Better watch her Mac; I'll take her from you yet."

"Oh, didn't I tell you?" Mac smiled, "You can have her. I'm trading her in for a younger one."

"Hmp!" Olie said letting Johni go to face Mac, "But will a younger one have you?" They all laughed and Johni reached over the counter to squeeze Mac's hand.

"What'll you have this fine morning, Johni?" Mac handed her the day's newspaper.

"How about hot tea and OJ," Johni answered accepting the paper.

"Coming right up, go, sit," Mac shooed her to her usual

table. She walked over and sat down at the back table nearest the phone. One of her favorite past times was people watching and from this vantage point she could sit and watch all day. Opening the paper she settled in to read about the previous day's events. No sooner had she started when Olie plopped herself in the chair opposite her. She sat for a moment waiting for Johni to acknowledge her. Johni smiled to herself but didn't lower the newspaper. After several long seconds Olie swept the newspaper out of her hands in one fluid motion.

"Olie," Johni mockingly whined, "What?!"

"There's this woman I want you to..." Olie started but before she could finish her sentence Johni already had her hands up.

"No Olie."

"Johni, come on she's really nice."

"They are all really nice. No!"

"This one is different," Olie stated defiantly. "She's older." Johni cocked her head to one side and eyeballed her friend.

"What do you mean she's older? What's that supposed to mean?" Being thirty years old, Johni wasn't sure by the way Olie said "older" just what "older" meant.

"Well," Olie said slowly, "older. You know more mature." Johni had to laugh out loud. Did this woman ever give up? She had to give her a break. Olie was trying so hard.

"Okay Olie, tell me about her." Olie sat up straighter and launched into one of her woman for acceptance pitches. More than anything in the world Olie wanted Johni to be happy which is why Johni put up with this. She loved her friend and knew that if nothing else she had good intentions.

"She's Italian of course," Olie started.

"Of course," Johni responded. For some unexplained reason being a minority was a requirement in Olie's book. She really wanted to hook her up with an African-American woman but Johni steered clear.

"You need a black woman Johni," Olie had explained once, "Black women know how to take care of a person." Couldn't argue with that, especially with a woman who was black herself.

"She's a very nice person and she's settled. Has herself together, you know, self-sufficient and very intelligent. Owns her own business, she does." Olie was trying too hard.

"Okay what's the catch?" Johni could hear a "but" coming a mile away.

"Nothing," Olie insisted, "You'd really like her." Johni considered for a moment. She had already gone this far, might as well go all the way.

"So when do I meet this new super woman?" Mac

finally made to the table with the tea and juice.

"In a few," Mac said setting down the cup and glass with a smile.

"Oh no, Mac, not you too," Johni groaned. Mac laughed and patted her on the shoulder.

"She really is very nice Johni." Looking from one to the other of her two friends Johni had the urge to run. Sighing out loud, as was a habit of hers, Johni conceded.

"Okay, I'll stay but do me a favor, don't hover." Olie beamed and Mac walked away laughing. She couldn't believe he was in on this. Johni just looked at them both and shook her head. Picking up her paper again Johni started about the business of trying to get through a whole article this time. She was about midway through a story about the Middle East when she heard Olie whisper, "There she is." Lowering the newspaper slowly as to not be obvious Johni almost fell out of her seat. There just inside the door, hugging Mac was Raven Michaels.

Seeing her again made Johni realize exactly why she hadn't been able to write this morning. This woman had been dancing around in her subconscious. She had a serious case of can't-get-that-woman-out-of-her-mind. She swallowed hard and made the decision to play it cool. She was not about to let some woman see her come unglued. She had a reputation to maintain. Not to mention the fact that Olie and Mac would never let her live it down.

Folding the newspaper neatly Johni stood as a beaming Mac led Raven to the table.

"Ms. Andrews," Raven said with surprise, "How nice to see you again."

"Hello," Johni smiled. "Please have a seat." As Raven sat Olie and Mac looked at each other confused.

"Again," Olie asked, "What do you mean again? You two know each other?"

"We met at a party last night," Johni offered. "How's your girlfriend?" Johni saw Olie wince. She had neglected to mention the girlfriend. At this point both Olie and Mac excused themselves. Raven sat up a little.

"Andi? She's okay. She's at work this morning." As she spoke Johni marveled at the softness of her voice. Somewhere, in the background, however, Johni thought she heard something else. What was it? It was almost as if Raven was hesitant in speaking of her girlfriend.

"Really? Where does she work?" Johni couldn't care less where, (what was her name?) Andi worked. She just wanted to hear Raven's voice. It really didn't matter what the subject was.

"At the mall. She works as a sales clerk for Learners." Raven cast her eyes down but not in shame. Johni saw a nervousness appear in Raven. Somehow Johni had expected the girlfriend of this woman to have a more professional job. Geez Johni, she thought. She couldn't help but wonder where such a shallow thought had come from. She decided to change the subject.

"And you? What do you do for a living," Johni asked. Raven smiled.

"You do get to the point don't you?" Suddenly Johni found herself doing something she rarely did, she started to apologize.

"I'm sorry. I didn't mean to be too forward." Johni couldn't believe that it was her own voice she was hearing. She'd always considered her steadfast forwardness a good trait.

"No not at all, it's refreshing to talk with someone who's not afraid to speak her mind." Raven looked up at her and Johni was positive that she would marry this woman. Never mind that Raven had a girlfriend, which was beside the point. Furthermore, cast aside the fact that Raven didn't even realize that Johni existed prior to twelve hours ago. This too was a meaningless fact. All that mattered now was that Johni had to convince this woman that she was falling madly in love with her.

"I work with computers." Johni knew that Raven was understating what she did for a living but that was okay. It had been a long time since she'd met anyone modest.

"Would you like something to drink?" Johni asked trying not to sound as eager as she felt. She didn't just want to get this woman a soda; she wanted to buy her a house.

"Sure, a soda will be fine." Johni looked up to catch Mac's attention but when she saw how busy he was with another customer she decided to get up and get it herself.

"Excuse me for a moment." As Johni got up, Raven checked her out for the first time. She had a strong body. She wasn't slim but sort of husky. She was calm and cool underneath, but Raven could sense a very sensitive person. Johni had taken great care in the image she projected. Raven liked that. She could also sense a real self-assuredness. This was another trait that Raven tended to admire in women. Strength. She found herself comparing Johni to Andi. Stop that she told herself it isn't fair. But she couldn't help it. Lately she compared every other woman she met to Andi. She tried not to but her relationship with Andi had become so trying these days. She use to think it was the age difference between them but now she realized that Andi was just plain selfish and mean. There had been many times, especially recently, when Andi had embarrassed her. She had taken to getting down right cruel at times. More and more Raven was beginning to realize that the relationship between her and Andi was going nowhere fast because Andi was so dependent. She would hardly let Raven out of her sight. And sometimes recently, Andi had done things that scared her a little. Cruel things.

Raven shook her head to clear her thoughts. She just didn't know what to do next. If only she could find someone who would be attentive to her needs. If only...Raven was stopped in mid-thought. She knew that she was gawking but it didn't matter, she couldn't believe what she was seeing.

"What?" Johni asked concerned about the surprise on Raven's face, "You don't like coke?" Raven looked up at Johni and after taking a second to regroup she shook her head.

"No, coke is fine." Johni smiled and set the glass down. Raven couldn't do anything but pull the glass to her and fish out one of the cherries.

* * *

The two of them sat there in Mac's and talked for three hours. They just didn't seem to run out of things to say. Johni found this woman intriguing. She was interesting and confident but not in an egotistical way. She was sure of herself and Johni liked that.

She listened, a skill very few people seemed to possess these days. Nothing was more irritating than spending time with a person who talked incisively about nothing. When it came time to leave Johni felt a slight tug on her heart, something she hadn't felt in a long time. She was enjoying this and didn't want it to end but she knew that she had to be realistic. She didn't chase women who were spoken for. Raven had someone. She had talked about Andi and maybe they were trying to work through their problems. That was okay. At the very least she'd made a wonderful new friend. That in itself was a beginning.

"Well," Raven said gathering her things, "I really need to get going. It's nearly noon and I do have work to do."

"Yeah, I need to get out of here too." It was weak but it was all she could think to say. She had desperately searched for something deep and mature but in the end she sounded lame. They stood up together and for one awkward moment Johni was unsure of what to do. It seemed as though Raven was unsure too.

"Thanks for the company. It was very nice getting to know you," Raven said taking Johni's hand. Suddenly Johni couldn't breathe. This woman's touch was incredible. It was so warm and soft. She looked up and the shine in Raven's eyes made her lose control for just a moment. Fighting to hide her immediate feelings Johni squeezed Raven's hand. After an awkward moment of silence Johni let go of her hand. Raven smiled and once again Johni found herself losing control.

"When can I see you again," She blurted out. Wanting to kick herself Johni could not believe she'd said that. Embarrassed she tried to back track to no avail.

"I mean, well, you can bring, oh hell!" She looked at

her feet. Raven was quiet for a moment and then giggled a little. She had that, "how cute" look on her face. Johni couldn't stand it. She felt stupid.

"How about tomorrow, here, same time." Johni looked up at Raven and after a couple of seconds, realizing with delight, that she was serious.

"Okay," was all Johni could say and with that Raven smiled and left. Johni stood there for a minute and marveled at how she was feeling. She was completely taken. Everything about this woman made her sit up and take notice. Obviously she wasn't alone in her observation others in the restaurant had noticed Raven as well. Now and then, during the course of their conversation, Johni had caught a side-glance of people staring at Raven in admiration. Turning to go back to the table for a bit she observed Olie staring at her, smiling.

"What?" Johni asked trying to sound irritated. But she just couldn't keep the smile out of her voice. Olie had her dead to rights and there was nothing Johni could do.

"Told you," Olie said following her to the table and taking the place across from her. "Didn't I tell you she was great?" Olie was tickled to death. She could hardly sit still.

"What you failed to mention was that she has a girlfriend. You breaking up relationships now Olie?" Olie looked slightly hurt but bounced back quickly.

"No," She defended, "they have a screwed up relationship. Andi Lancaster is mean. Raven needs someone who will be kind to her.

"Mean? Mean how?" Johni didn't like the sound of that.

"Mean." Olie restated, "She doesn't have much regard for Raven that's all. She needs someone like you."

"Like me? How do you know what I'm like Olie?"

"You're kind, considerate and compassionate Johni. You're a people person. Hell, what's to know? You wear your damn heart on your sleeve," Olie scolded. She was getting frustrated as she always did, with Johni's excuses for herself. Johni considered only for a moment what it would be like to be with Raven before she cautioned herself. This was ridiculous.

"I'm not going to date a woman with a girlfriend and that is final!" Olie smiled a knowing smile that made Johni's stomach turn a little.

"Too late," Olie said as she got up and started toward the counter. Had she been listening when they had made their date for tomorrow? All Johni needed was for everyone to know she was chasing a married woman. (were they married?) Johni favored her

* * *

Raven walked to her MG Midget, got in and drove

away without looking back. After two or three blocks she let out the breath she'd been holding for the past five minutes. What the hell was she doing telling that woman she'd see her again? Was she nuts? Raven always prided herself on being faithful and true to the person she was with. Sure she was human and every now and then a beautiful woman with long legs would catch her eye but all she ever did was look. But Johni Andrews wasn't exactly what one would consider tall. She was taller than Raven but just about everyone was. Enmeshed in thought, Raven came out of her daze just in time to see a truck pull out in front of her barely missing the front end of her car. Swerving to avoid getting hit, Raven shot the driver of the truck a nasty look. He flipped her the finger and she couldn't resist smiling at him, which of course just served to anger him more, which made her feel much better. Maneuvering the car off the road into a parking lot Raven switched off the engine and sat back. She needed to take a moment to think about this.

As mad as she was at the truck driver for pulling out in front of her she had to admit that she could have been paying more attention. Again her mind wondered back to Johni Andrews. She liked that name. It had a nice ring to it. It fit the woman's personality. She seemed so bold and a bit cocky. It was a nice change from "Andi the spineless". No, she told herself, you can't do this. You have Andi. Did she though? Did she have Andi or did Andi have her? This was a question that she'd often pondered lately.

She was always taking care of Andi. She was responsible for everything in their lives; shopping, paying bills, and lately, even footing the bills. She was there when Andi wanted to talk, cry or scream. She never asked for anything for herself. Raven didn't feel as though she could. Raven knew that Andi either couldn't or wouldn't be relied upon. How could she? She spent so much time leaning on everybody else. It was like having a teenage boy with a bad temper around the house. Andi lumbered around eating junk food and drinking beer whenever she was home. She couldn't hold a ten-minute conversation with Andi without getting upset. All of this made for an extremely lonely existence for Raven. She had no one to air her complaints to. She had no one to hold her and tell her that things would be okay. A couple, laughing and holding hands, walked across the parking lot in front of the car. Raven just shook her head as she envisioned having the same kind of relationship. She wanted to laugh and enjoy the time she spent with people, especially the person she'd chosen to spend the rest of her life with. She couldn't remember the last time she and Andi had laughed like that.

"The things we get ourselves into," she whispered

quietly. With a tired deep sigh Raven started the car and headed home.

* * *

At 4:30 p.m. Johni was at home writing feverishly when the phone rang. It was strange but after breakfast this morning she had come home and felt so inspired that she'd written eighteen pages. That was amazing considering that she usually gave herself a goal of six pages a day. Although all of the writing had made her tired she wasn't complaining it paid the bills. She was slightly annoyed now that the phone was ringing. She let the machine pick it up and listened as the call was answered.

"Hi, this is me. I'm not able to come to the phone right now which means I'm either not home, been hit by a car or am writing. At any rate leave a message. I'll get back to you."

B-E-E-P

"Johni, its Olie." (Johni sighed, what now?) "I need your permission to give out your phone number." (Hell no!) "I know that you usually don't give it out but Raven...." Johni lunged for the receiver.

"What?!" Johni almost yelled into the phone, "What did Raven say?"

"Damn girl, hang on a minute, she's right here."

"Olie, No, Wait!"

"Johni?" The soft voice on the other end of the line was unmistakably Raven's.

"Hi. How are you?" Johni managed. She was going to kill Olie.

"Fine. Listen there's this theater club on the west side and a friend of mine is in the play they are putting on tonight, want to go?" There, Raven thought, I did it, now she'll say no and I can go on with my life.

"Sure, what time?" Johni's heart was racing a mile a minute.

"About seven?" Raven couldn't believe she'd said yes.

"Okay, do you want to meet at Mac's?" Johni's mind kept screaming, ask her if her girlfriend's coming but her mouth just wouldn't respond.

"Okay," Raven answered sheepishly. Then as if reading Johni's mind, "It'll be just me and you." Johni took in a sharp breath and hoped that Raven hadn't heard her.

"Okay, I'll see you at seven than." Johni had to get off the phone before she exploded.

"I'll see you then." Raven said and with that she hung up the phone. Johni forgot all about killing Olie. Right now she just wanted to kiss her. She couldn't believe Raven had called. She could hardly contain her excitement. It felt like she was in high school again. Checking the time, Johni saw that it was 4:40.

"That gives me two hours and fifteen minutes," she

surmised out loud. Smiling, Johni headed for the shower.

* * *

Raven stood in front of the mirror for the ninth time in two hours. After Johni had said yes she'd rushed home, saw Andi off to work, thank God the mall stayed open until eleven, took a shower, and systematically tried on everything in her closet. She felt silly. What the hell difference did it make, they were just friends. (Yeah right) Finally settling on a navy blue jumpsuit that she was positive she looked good in Raven went to the kitchen and poured herself a glass of wine. She seldom drank much but it would calm her nerves. She had thirty minutes before she was to meet Johni and Mac's was only fifteen minutes away; she had timed the drive home. Sitting down at the breakfast bar she took a sip from her glass.

"I can't believe I'm doing this," she said out loud to no one. Laughing she took another drink, "Great, now I'm talking to myself." Checking her watch, Raven realized that only two minutes had passed. This was going to be the longest thirty minutes of her life, she was sure of it.

Chapter 3

Johni stood back and offered her hand to help Raven from the car. If she was trying to impress Raven she was doing a wonderful job. When Raven had arrived at Mac's she was pleased to see Johni already there. (She hated to wait.) Even more pleasing was that Johni seemed impressed by what Raven was wearing. She had stood back and looked at Raven in a way that no one else had in a very long time. She then made it known by raising one eyebrow and saying "Damn you look nice." Raven loved that Johni was so well, so cocky. When they left Johni had insisted on taking her car. It was obvious that she had just had it washed and waxed. Johni walked Raven around the jeep and opened the door for her. Raven was impressed. On the way to the theater they had made nervous small talk. At the theater door Johni again stood back for Raven to go first. All Raven could do was look at her and smile.

"What?" Johni asked once they were inside.

"What do you mean?" Raven responded. Most people hated that about her. She tended to act like there was no question knowing damn well there was. Johni, however, just seemed amused with the game. She liked that.

"What are you smiling about?"

"Nothing in particular." Raven couldn't help but giggle.

"No really, I want to know what you're thinking," Johni

pushed. Raven could see by her determination that she wasn't going to be put off.

"I don't know," Raven started, "It's just so nice to have someone be so attentive." Johni saw an opportunity here.

"Andi isn't? Attentive I mean." Johni looked Raven straight in the eye when she asked that and Raven knew that she'd never be able to lie to this woman.

"No, not really," Raven answered dropping her head slightly. Johni took her hand and led her gently towards the theater.

"Well then, it's a good thing I came along isn't it." She smirked slightly and Raven laughed.

The play was wonderful. Raven wasn't sure if it were the play that was so intriguing or the fact that Johni had really seemed to appreciate the show. Andi hated things like this. She'd sit and fidget through the whole thing. The difference with Johni was that as interested as she had seemed to be in the play she would make a point to look over at Raven or touch her hand only for a moment as if to let her know that she was there. Afterwards as they stood outside the theater Raven couldn't help but stare at Johni. There seemed to be so much she wanted to ask her. She really hated for the evening to end.

"What time do you have to be home?" Johni asked looking at Raven in a way that made her feel almost naked.

"What time is it?" Johni had to smile as she looked at

her watch.

"What?" Raven asked seeing the smile. Johni just wanted to hug her.

"I think that's cute."

"What's cute?" Raven asked again smiling bigger. Damn, the way this woman made her feel was incredible!

"You ask me what time it is although you are wearing a watch. It's cute." Raven had to laugh. She was aware that she did that, however no one else had ever noticed before or bothered to point it out if they had.

"Does that bother you?" Raven asked with a coy little smile. Johni knew what she was doing.

"You're fishing." Raven didn't know what to say. She hadn't expected to be called on that. She laughed and turned away.

"Oh my goodness, you are cocky aren't you." She hadn't meant to say that. Johni just smiled.

"Cocky? Is that what you think I am?"

"I don't mean it in a bad way. It's nice. I like it," Raven said out loud in her mind she admitted that it was a turn on." Thankfully, it was too dark for Johni to see her embarrassment for that thought.

"Well thank you."

"So? What time is it?" Raven asked laughing. Johni looked at her watch again.

"10:00."

"Well, I guess I should be getting back," Raven said dropping her head slightly. Johni stepped towards her and with one finger lifted her head back up.

"You are just too damn beautiful to do that," Johni said with a smile.

Raven was surprised and pleased.

"Do what?" She asked returning the smile only slightly embarrassed.

"To drop your head like that. You have a lot of class lady, keep your head up." Johni dropped her hand and smiled again. Raven was having a very hard time controlling her feelings. She had the urge to grab this woman and hold on for dear life. Johni was so cool though. Raven wished that she could read her mind.

"Thank you," was all Raven could say.

On the drive back to Mac's they were both quiet, pondering what the other might be thinking. However, neither of them asked. Once they were at Mac's Johni walked Raven to her car and asked for her keys.

"Why?" Raven asked. Johni had to laugh.

"Just give me the keys." Raven handed her keys over not altogether sure why.

Johni took the keys with a smile, turned and unlocked the car door. Opening the door she stood back for Raven to get in. Raven just stood there awestruck. This woman was unbelievable. It was like a dream.

"Thank you," Was all Raven could squeeze out of her vocabulary. Johni smiled, gave her a nod then stepped back for Raven to get in. Raven turned and gave Johni a quick hug as she approached the open door.

"Thank you for coming," Raven said as she reluctantly let go.

"Anytime," Johni responded.

"We still on for breakfast tomorrow?" Raven asked hoping that she didn't sound as eager as she felt. Johni smiled.

"Sure, what time." Raven did a fast run in her head of what tomorrow held in way of a schedule.

"Is nine okay?"

"Sure, I'll see you there at nine." Johni smiled and Raven didn't want to leave.

"You'd better go," Johni prompted.

"You trying to get rid of me?" Raven asked feigning hurt. Johni reached out and touched Raven's hand.

"No, never." With that she turned and walked back to her jeep. Getting in she waited until she saw Raven close the door of her car. She then waved and pulled her own vehicle out of the lot and headed home.

* * *

Johni locked the garage door and went into the house. Walking to the computer she sat down. After watching the

Windows screen saver for a bit she tapped the mouse and let herself into her journal. Johni spent the next hour and a half writing down every thought that occurred to her about Raven Crandall. She didn't even look up until she had filled fifteen pages. She knew that she was in trouble. She had fallen in love. It had caught her off guard and now there wasn't a damn thing she could do about it. Tonight, while they had been together she had put on a cool demeanor all the while coming unglued inside. She'd had the urge to hug her many times as well as the need to just stand some place holding this woman. She felt an almost desperate need to protect Raven. Johni laughed out loud. Damn! What have I done here? She asked herself out loud. The silence of the house mocked her as she sat there rereading the things she'd wrote.

Everything about Raven intrigued her. The whole world brightened in her presence. She loved to hear her laugh, to see her smile. During the play, there were several times when Johni had, in fact, reached over and patted Raven's hand or smiled at her. She had wanted to make sure that Raven knew she was there if she needed her. She hadn't seemed to mind. It wasn't like it had been before with Brenda. Brenda had hated for her to touch her in public. She was always afraid someone would see them. Johni hadn't felt like this in a very long time. Closing out her journal for the night Johni got up and went to shower. As she stood letting the water run over her body, she thought of Raven and what it would be like to be with her right now. She could almost smell her. She had noticed the first time she had ever been close to her how wonderful Raven had smelled. Toweling off she got into bed suddenly feeling very lonely. She looked at the phone and realized that she didn't have Raven's number. Turning her back to the phone she decided that she'd have to get it tomorrow. She wasn't sure exactly how she would pull off talking to her on the phone chancing Andi finding out but that didn't matter now. She just needed to know that she could reach Raven if the need arose.

* * *

Raven knew that she should go straight home but she felt good and she wanted to drive a bit. Driving was something she enjoyed a great deal and when she was feeling good she always felt the need to let go on the road. The cool night air felt good as Raven drove out onto the old highway and let the MG go. Approaching 120 mph she let off the gas and coasted a while. Stopping at the top of Reman's Hill, Raven got out and stood looking down at the lights of the town. Where had Johni Andrews been all her life? Was this woman for real? She had to know but she was afraid to find out. This woman had the potential to really break her heart and Raven knew it. She had had such a good time tonight. She really hated to go home and let Andi screw it up. She knew that Andi would end up making a mockery of the night by ending it on a sour note. It was as if Andi couldn't help it.

She loved Andi, she really did but Andi was so selfish. Sure she opened doors for Raven and took her out once in a while but it was forced and Raven knew it. In fact, now that she'd seen Johni in action she was sure of it. Loving someone should be natural. Andi was so involved with herself she hardly had time for Raven. Andi couldn't help it though and Raven understood that.

"Oh listen to me," she said out loud, "I've become the make-an-excuse-for-Andi kid." Looking at her watch Raven decided she'd better head home. No point in making things worse. She hesitated for just one more look at the lights of the town and couldn't help but think of how wonderful it would be to have shared this with Johni.

All of the lights in the house were on when Raven pulled into the driveway. She turned the car and the headlights off at the same time. She knew that it wouldn't be wise to sit here for long so she took a deep breath and laid her head back against the seat for a moment. She hated this feeling of not knowing what happens next. She should be able to look forward to coming home but instead she dreaded it. Raven hated the idea of having to face Andi after having such a wonderful time with Johni. She knew, however, that it was unavoidable. While she sat considering the best approach a curtain moved in the front window.

"Damn," Raven whispered to the night. Now she knew that she was in for a confrontation. Andi was waiting and no doubt willing to argue. It would be okay if Andi could say what was on her mind and then storm off mad but she never did. There was almost always some kind of physical confrontation. Opening the car door slowly, Raven got out, straightened her clothes and prepared for the worse.

* * *

"What do you mean you went to a play? You went by yourself?" Andi was already starting to get red in the face. Raven had gotten exactly what she had suspected she would. As Raven walked through the door she noticed that Andi had positioned herself so that the first thing Raven saw would be her. Arms folded, face stern, Andi was ready for a fight.

"A play Andi, I just went to a play. Does this have to get difficult?" Home five minutes and she already wanted to leave again.

"Raven, you don't even like going anywhere by yourself." Andi was getting angrier and now Raven was frustrated. Andi was winding up.

"Why do you always have to be suspicious whenever I

go out alone? Can't I be alone once in a while?" Raven knew she was wrong for leading Andi to believe that she had gone by herself but it made her so mad when Andi acted like this. Besides it was none of her business who she spent time with. Since Andi couldn't act right how could she blame her for wanting a nice evening out?

"Why couldn't you have waited until I could go with you? Andi whined. Raven really hated that. Andi whined a lot and at times Raven would get the urge to tell her to grow up. But she knew it would just make things worse if she told her that. Andi hated being accused of acting like a child. She seemed to have an inferior complex about how others saw her.

"Andi, you don't even like plays."

"I do too!" Andi shouted. "There you go again acting like you're better than I am!" Oh God, Raven thought, and here we go again.

"Andi I do not."

"Yes you do! You always act like you're some high-class chick. You're no better than I am!" Andi stood up. Raven readied herself.

"Andi, I don't want to do this now. I'm going to bed." Raven turned towards the hallway and Andi stepped in front of her.

"Not until you tell me who you were with!" Raven stood there for a moment looking at this woman that she was supposed to love. The only emotions she could muster up now were pity and disgust. Johni, she thought, would never do this.

"Andi get out of my way, I'm not going to fight with you tonight. I'm tired and I'm going to bed." Raven tried to step past and Andi shoved her. Raven knew that she shouldn't react but she'd be damned if someone thought that they could shove her for no reason, especially someone who claimed to love her. She shoved back. Andi raised her hand as if to strike Raven across the face.

"That'll be the last fucking move you make!" Raven was mad. She hated using that kind of language but lately it seemed all Andi understood. Now she was pissed for two reasons; Andi was being an ass and she had allowed Andi to provoke her.

"What are you going to do?" Andi laughed mocking Raven, which only served to make Raven lose more control. Andi always alluded to the fact that Raven was smaller than she was as if that made a difference.

"Get out of my way!" Raven, almost on the verge of tears, screamed. This coupled with the look in her eyes made Andi suddenly back off. Raven pushed past her and went into the bedroom, locking the door behind her. She wondered if Andi would let it go this time or if she would end up busting the door down like last time. It had taken her two days to fix Andi's handy work. Leaning against the door Raven let the tears go. Damn! Why did it have to be like this? After four years you'd think something would have changed but it only seems to get worse.

When they had first met Andi had been a wonderful companion. But, as time passed and Andi had opened up to her about a depraved childhood, Andi's demeanor changed. It was as if she felt she could abuse Raven because she had listened. It was crazy. Letting herself slip down the door to the floor Raven sat and had a good cry. She seemed to be doing a lot more of that lately. After about five minutes of really good tears Raven let her mind regroup itself. One thing she refused to do was to feel sorry for herself. Getting up she went to the shower. Allowing the water get as hot as her skin could stand it, Raven showered as the water washed a bit of the tension away. Her mind wandered back to Johni. She wondered what she was doing right now. Was she thinking about her? Letting her mind wander, Raven envisioned Johni in the shower with her. She smiled to herself as she imagined what Johni's nude body would look like. It was obvious that she had strong shoulders. Raven liked that. She pictured them standing there face to face, the water running over their bodies. She felt Johni's hands as they moved expertly over her entire body, feeling and tugging at all of the right spots. Raven felt that familiar yearning deep within her start to stir. She moved her own hand down her body; slowly fantasizing that it was Johni's. She placed it between her legs searching as she knew Johni would.

Although she knew nothing of Johni's lovemaking abilities she surmised that she was probably incredible. Moving in time with her own rhythm, Raven pleasured herself all the while feeling not her own hands but Johni's. She climaxed in a relatively short time. This was unusual for her. It was just one more way in which she could tell that she was deprived of the real love she deserved. Breathless, she leaned against the shower wall still feeling Johni's hands on her. Damn it! She thought turning off the water. Although she felt momentarily satisfied she knew that what she'd just done was going to make it worse for her. It was bad enough that Johni stayed in her thoughts but now she was in her fantasies too? Toweling off Raven had to smile. Showering would just never feel the same from now on. She shook her head and laughed out loud. She covered her mouth just in case Andi was nearby. She couldn't believe that this woman was having this kind of effect on her.

"Raven?" It was Andi jarring Raven back to reality.

"What?" She asked with annoyance.

"Can I come in?" Andi was crying. She always did. She did and said things that were really hurtful only to fall apart and apologize fifteen minutes later. It was like being on a roller coaster. Raven considered not letting her in for a fleeting moment. Finally, walking to the door Raven turned the lock.

"It's open," she said walking away. Andi pushed the door slowly open as if she were expecting Raven to throw something at her. Raven hated that too, she would never do anything like that but when Andi came to say how sorry she was she always acted as if Raven were someone to be afraid of. This only served to fuel Raven's anger yet again.

"Raven, I'm really sorry," Andi whined. "If you want to go to plays by yourself you can." Oh great, Raven thought, she's giving me permission, the nerve...

"I just get so insecure," Andi was going on, "I wish that you enjoyed those things with me. You always seem to..." Andi went on talking but Raven tuned her out. Johni would never give her this, she thought. I'll bet Johni would have swooped me up and carried me to the bedroom as soon as I had shut the door behind me.

"Raven? Are you listening to me?" Suddenly jolted from what was becoming another promising fantasy, Raven braced herself to make an all too familiar speech. She, of course, had two conversations, one on the outside and one on the inside.

"Of course I'm listening to you Andi. (Bullshit!) It's okay, I understand. (Yeah right.) Let's just leave it alone and go to bed. (You can sleep in Alaska)" Raven smiled in spite of herself. Andi thought that she was smiling at her.

"Great Raven! Let's go to bed." Raven still couldn't believe after all these years that Andi could still go from total depression to totally normal, (Whatever that happened to be for Andi) in less than a few minutes. She gave her obligatory kiss to Andi, got into bed and turned over to go to sleep. Andi got undressed, climbed into bed and turned her back to Raven as well. Raven's last thought before going to sleep was that she would be willing to bet that Johni would never turn her back on her in bed or otherwise.

Chapter 4

At 4:07 a.m. Johni was wide-awake. She lay in bed for close to an hour before she gave in and got up. Putting on some tea she sat down at the computer and stared at the blank screen. Sleep was refusing to come. Tossing and turning was not something she often experienced. And over a woman? That was really bad. She wondered if Raven was thinking of her. Looking at the clock Johni surmised that she had about five hours before she had to meet Raven for breakfast. Watching the clock, she thought, how pathetic. Turning on the computer she settled in to do some writing.

* * *

Andi stirred in her sleep. Awake at 4:30am Raven watched Andi sleep. How could someone so pretty be so ugly inside? She loved her. Raven was very comfortable with the fact that she really did love Andi. She just didn't have a lot of strength left to deal with all of the crap. There had been a time when all of the ugliness hadn't been so apparent. It was funny how things could completely escape someone in love. You believe something about a person and when the veil is lifted and reality sets in everything goes to shit. It was within the past three years or so that things seemed to worsen. She reached out and touched Andi's cheek. Andi opened her eyes. It surprised Raven; she hadn't expected her to wake up. She smiled despite her thoughts.

"I love you, Raven." Raven moved over and softly hugged her.

"I love you too."

"Raven, don't leave me." Andi pleaded. "I couldn't make it without you." Raven sighed quietly. Somewhere in her heart she believed that breaking up would definitely have a devastating effect on Andi.

"I won't, Andi, don't worry honey." Andi settled into Raven's arms and went back to sleep. Raven lay holding her stroking her hair for a long time. Sometimes Andi was like a child. She appeared to need protection from the cruel world outside. She brought out the nurturing in Raven. Finally she realized she had no choice. Although she had a very strong attraction for Johni, she was where she needed to be. Johni was strong but Andi...Andi needed her. Deciding that she would back away from this thing with Johni before it became more serious she got up to take a shower. As the water ran over her body she couldn't help but feel sad. Who knew what could have become of her and Johni. She had definitely felt something special. Was she making the right decision? Was Andi's happiness more important than her own? She couldn't be selfish. Andi needed her and as long as Andi needed her she would stay with her. She'd made a commitment. She had made a promise; a promise she had to keep.

* * *

At 9:10 a.m. Raven still hadn't shown up. Johni was antsy. She kept watch on the door and every time it opened sounding the little bell hanging in the corner Johni jumped. Mac was keeping her glass of OJ full. He kept a watchful eye on her. He had never seen her so eager for anything. He constantly smiled at her and it was making her self-conscious. She'd read through the newspaper twice but still no Raven. Johni couldn't help jerking her head up to look when the door opened. If she kept this up she'd get whip-lash. Olie was watching from behind the counter, which only served to make Johni even more nervous. At 9:20 Johni started to worry. At 9:30 she realized that Raven wasn't coming. Getting up from the table Johni paid her bill and left. She didn't say anything to anyone and no one said anything to her.

She had been stood up for the very first time in her life. Starting the Jeep Johni decided to drive by Raven's house. She had pulled out into the street when she realized that she had no clue as to where Raven lived. Stopping at a red light she tried to come up with an alternate plan. I'll call her, she thought to herself. Nope, can't do that either, no phone number. "Damn!" Johni shouted. A man in the truck next to her glanced over and she gave him a go-to-hell look. She could not believe how let down she was feeling. She had never let a woman set her up like that. She always called the shots. She wasn't supposed to fall in love with Raven; Raven was supposed to fall in love with her. For years now, ever since the breakup with Brenda, Johni had prided herself on not falling for anyone. It was safer that way. She didn't have to invest any emotions. Until now she had managed to stay on track. Raven Michaels was different though. This woman had all of the control. Johni didn't like that at all and could kick herself for letting it happen. She drove past home and turned to go up towards Reman's Hill. She needed to deal with this newfound emotion she was experiencing. She was angry...no that wasn't true, it wasn't anger she was feeling. She was hurt.

* * *

Raven sat at the breakfast nook and watched the clock. She had already decided not to meet Johni for breakfast. It was just too risky. She could not afford to find this woman any more attractive than she already had. Even after deciding this morning to cut off any budding passions she still found herself thinking constantly of Johni Andrews. She had to remove herself from the path of this hurricane.

Andi had left in a fairly decent mood. Raven's stating that she wouldn't leave had given her reassurance. Now at ten till nine Raven was about as unsure of that statement as she could ever be. She'd cleaned the living room, did the dishes, restocked soda in the fridge and cleaned her office. Now she had simply run out of things to do. She knew that it was wrong to just not show. She owed Johni more than that. Raven was scared though. What if she saw Johni and couldn't help herself? She didn't feel in control of the situation or her feelings and she didn't like that. Helping herself to her forth cup of coffee,(she'd surely be wired all day now) she walked to the phone. She doesn't have my phone number, Raven thought. Disappointed that she hadn't given it to Johni, Raven looked longingly at the phone. What would she do when Raven didn't show up? The grandfather clock in the foyer struck the hour of nine. Raven grabbed her keys and ran out the door.

She wasn't at Mac's. Raven was extremely disappointed. At the last minute she had decided to meet Johni after all. By the time she got the crazy garage door opener to work, warmed up the car and made it through the early morning traffic it was 9:32 a.m. when she reached Mac's. She didn't go in but stood and looked in the window. Johni was nowhere in sight. Raven wanted to cry. Why had she waited so long to go? Of course Johni left, after all Raven was a half hour late. She couldn't expect someone to wait that long. Johni couldn't have known that she had been sitting in the nook stressing. She didn't have Johni's phone number with her and quite frankly she was too embarrassed to ask Olie for it. They would no doubt know that she had stood Johni up. Damn, was all she could say as she pulled her car around to head home. At the four-way stop she decided that home was the last place she wanted to be. Slipping the MG into gear Raven headed for Reman's Hill.

* * *

Johni stood on the hill and took in the scene from below. She loved it here on Reman's. It was so peaceful. There had been many times in the past when something really heavy would weigh on her mind and Johni would come here to ponder life's questions. This was where she usually brought her tears for release. There was something about the idea of being up here, above the problems of the town and its inhabitants. Although today there were no tears it sure felt like there could have been. She couldn't figure out why this woman's standing her up was hurting so much. She had been truly disappointed. On the drive up she felt empty. This was ridiculous. She couldn't possibly feel this strongly after so short a time. Hell if she felt this way now maybe being stood up was a good thing. Maybe she couldn't have afforded to invest anymore of her heart in this. Picking up a rock she stepped to the edge of the hill and tossed it as far as she could. She wished that right now she could toss her heart right along with it. In the distance she could hear a car climbing rather quickly up the hill. Oh hell, she thought, I really didn't want any company.

* * *

Raven's heart leaped to her throat. She couldn't believe what she was seeing. There at the top of Reman's was Johni Andrews, standing bigger than life with this really surprised look on her face. Here! On her hill! Fate, Raven thought, this has to be fate. God wanted me to be here, I just know that He did. Raven couldn't breathe. Pulling onto the small out crop at the top of the hill, Raven cut the engine off but didn't get out. Would Johni be angry? She was standing, sunglasses hiding her eyes, leaning up against the Jeep. From where she was sitting she couldn't read Johni's eyes. Johni stood there briefly then walked over, opened Raven's car door and offered her a hand. Raven smiled and gently put her hand in Johni's. It felt so warm and strong. She was pulled to her feet easily and she marveled at the strength she felt in that action.

Unexpectedly, Raven felt herself being pulled even further into Johni's arms. She couldn't stop it and she didn't want to. As she let herself be gathered up into this woman's arms she released all her inhibitions. They stood there on the Hill shamelessly absorbed in each other.

Raven felt the definition of Johni's chest and arms. Slipping her arms around Johni's neck Raven could feel the strength in her shoulders. She could take me, Raven thought, if she wanted to. Suddenly the rest of the world ceased to exist.

Johni held Raven tight against her body as if she were hanging on for dear life. Neither of them said a word as they stood there holding each other. After what seemed like only seconds, Johni loosened her hold on Raven slightly and Raven wanted to scream, no don't. Looking up into Johni's face she saw something she hadn't seen in a very long time. True, honest, pure love. Raven felt humbled at the look in Johni's eyes as she turned to look away. Johni stopped her with one hand on her chin. Tilting Raven's face up, Johni kissed her lips in such a passionate way that the very ground on which they were standing seemed to melt away. Raven, at first taken aback, responded with just as strong a passion. She took Johni by surprise as her tongue probed Johni's mouth in a hungry, deep but gentle way. Although it was difficult, Johni pulled back and again gathered Raven into her arms.

"I thought you changed your mind," Johni whispered into Raven's ear. Raven had to smile.

"I did," she said with the sexiest smile she could muster up. Johni leaned back without letting go of Raven.

"What?"

"I did change my mind but before I knew it I'd changed it back," Raven said laughing. Johni laughed with her and then something occurred to her.

"Wait a minute, what are you doing here." Raven smiled.

"What are you doing here?" She asked.

"I come here to think sometimes," Johni answered.

"Me too," Raven said snuggling into Johni closer. "Must be fate." Johni couldn't believe this. She felt so complete with this woman in her arms. She was about to kiss her again when Raven pulled back. Letting go Raven stepped back a couple of feet.

"This isn't right Johni," she said looking down at her feet. "I'm with someone." Johni joined her in looking down. She didn't have any answers.

"I know," was all she could say. She knew somehow that Raven would feel this way and she couldn't begrudge her that. She loved this woman and all she knew was that whatever happened would be all right with her as long as they were together somehow. The rest would be only minor details.

"What do you want me to do?" Johni asked. It appeared that the ball was in Raven's court. Johni wasn't sure she liked that.

"I don't know," Raven answered obviously perplexed. Johni felt a strong tug at her heart. She wanted to hold

Raven but knew it would only make things worse.

"I've got to go," Raven said turning to her car.

"Okay," Johni answered quietly. She just didn't know what to do. She walked Raven over to the car. Raven turned and hugged Johni. Both their hearts ached.

"When will I see you again?" Johni had to ask. Raven squeezed her hand.

"I don't know." With that Raven got into her car, glanced back once and left Johni standing on top of Reman's Hill alone.

Chapter 5

Raven tried for the next twenty-four hours to not call Johni. Leaving Johni on the Hill was one of the hardest things she'd had ever done but she knew that it had been necessary. She just couldn't let this thing go any further. When she made a commitment she kept it. And she had made a commitment to Andi. When they first met Andi hadn't seemed so dependent but now Raven was sure that if she left, it would destroy Andi. She couldn't be responsible for that.... not again. Raven's mind wandered back to another time and another relationship.

She hadn't always lived the gay life. Once she had lived a straight life. She had tried her best to be a good wife to a man who had deserved much more than a wife who couldn't love him in the way he needed. In the end, though, she had to answer to the natural calling of who she really was. Raven was a lesbian and there came a time when she just couldn't deny it anymore. After 11 years of marriage that time came and a lot of people ended up hurt. Walker Davidson had been a wonderful man. Nothing had hurt her more than denying him the one thing that would make his life complete. Her.

During their marriage he had been very understanding. He knew who she was inside and he realized her torture. Walker had even taken Raven to her first gay club. He did everything he could to make things easy on her. Even to the point of looking the other way if she had needed to spend time with a woman. Although it hurt him, he always understood and did whatever he could to help Raven be who she was. Finally after watching her yearn for the lesbian lifestyle she needed for so long, Walker did the most unselfish thing anyone could do for the person they loved. He let her go.

Tears ran down Raven's face as she remembered the day they had reached the decision that she would move out. They talked. They cried but in the end they remained best friends. Even after they had been apart for a while he would still come by and check on her. Raven knew that she was forever under his watchful eye. He would always protect her. And sometimes when no one else was around Walker would lean over and hug her lightly, whispering, "You know I still love you."

Two years ago Walker died. He had a heart attack and after lingering for a month he quietly slipped into a place where Raven was sure he was at peace. The tears flowed as Raven wished she could talk to Walker now. His death had left Raven with emptiness. She had lost her best friend and at times like this she really needed him. He had known Andi before his death and liked her enough. However, Raven knew in her heart that Walker had never really taken her relationship with Andi seriously. He would have liked Johni. She stubbornly dried her tears. Look at me, she thought, I'm a mess. She would not be responsible for pain like that again. Granted Andi was no comparison to Walker but still hurting her would be an awful thing to do. And who knew how she would react. Walker was a strong man and he had a hard time. What would Andi do if she left her? How would she survive? Andi really did love her, of that Raven was sure. That was it, Andi needed her and she would stay.

Raven picked up the morning newspaper to throw it out and there underneath was the program to the theater show she had gone to with Johni. Damn, she thought as she picked up the program. Determination to stay with Andi was suddenly being undermined by a simple play program. She missed Johni as if they'd been apart for weeks. She couldn't believe that they had just seen each other yesterday. What was she going to do? Andi had come home last night with flowers and a bottle of wine. It had been really nice and while they had shared that wine she had fought hard to keep Johni out of her thoughts. It worked, for a while. After the second glass of wine she couldn't help but think about Johni and wish it were them here instead of her and Andi. She'd felt guilty but she couldn't help it. After the wine they had gone to bed and Andi had wanted to make love. Raven went through the motions but her heart was truly somewhere else. She felt guilt in the highest degree. She'd slept restless and woke up in a horrible mood. Andi was of course oblivious to any of Raven's mood swings. She had kissed her this morning and skipped off to work as if nothing was wrong. So what else was new. She'd be willing to bet Johni wouldn't have done that. She had to stop doing that.

She found herself comparing the two of them more and more and that wasn't good. Nor was it fair. Andi seemed to be losing in every comparison. Raven looked at the clock over the nook, 3:47 p.m. She wanted to call Johni just to hear her voice. Maybe, that wouldn't be so bad. It wouldn't be like she was seeing her or anything. She'd just say hi, make sure that her "friend" was okay. She could do that, there would be no harm. She went into her office and looked for the phone number. She knew she had it. Olie had given it to her after they had called about the play. Finally after tearing the office apart, Raven picked up the phone and called Mac's.

"Mac's," answered the voice on the other end of the line. Raven recognized Olie.

"Olie? It's Raven."

"Hey girl! What's up?" Olie asked. She always had a way of making Raven feel at ease from the first couple of words in conversation. Raven had to smile.

"Nothing, but I need a favor. I need Johni Andrews's phone number." Raven waited. She knew that Olie would milk this but right now it didn't matter, she just needed to talk to Johni.

"Her phone number huh?" Olie asked slyly. "Didn't I give you that?" Raven knew that Olie would give her the number just as soon as they finished their dance.

"I misplaced it Olie, come on don't give me a hard time, just the number," Raven said in a mock plead.

"So you like her huh?" Olie asked. She just wasn't going to let this go.

"Yes, I like her. Now can I have the number please?"

"All right, hold on I'll go get it. It's in the office," as Olie went to retrieve the phone number Raven felt butterflies in her stomach. She was going to talk to her, actually hear her voice. This excited her.

"I can't find it," came Olie's voice suddenly back on the line.

"What do you mean you can't find it?" Look for it." Raven demanded. She heard herself talking but could not believe that it was actually her.

"Calm down child," Olie laughed, "I have it; I was just messin with you. Damn, you are smitten." Raven was suddenly embarrassed.

"Oh Olie, I'm so sorry. I didn't mean that the way it sounded. Can you ever forgive me?" She felt really stupid.

"Oh Raven, please, forgive hell, if I were in love with someone like that I wouldn't want anyone messin with me either." In love? Did she say, in love?

"I'm not in love with Johni," Raven stated.

"Girl please," Olie laughed, "It is definitely love." Was that true? Was she falling in love with Johni? Oh Lord, Raven thought, she really was. Damn!

"The number, Olie." Olie gave her the phone number, said her good-byes, giggling the whole time, and hung up. Raven sat there at the nook for a long time going over and over her feelings. Love? She had seen that word fleetingly in her mind a couple of times but had not stopped to take it seriously. Now, because of what Olie had said she had to stop and think about it. Love? Now that she thought about it she had to consider it. After a time she put it aside. She could spend all day pondering what she felt but it wasn't going to get her talking to Johni any quicker and right now that was what she truly needed. After dialing the phone number she let it ring once and hung up. Her heart was racing. What made her do that? Suddenly she had become really anxious? No, it wasn't fear that she was feeling but excitement, over excitement. Making a conscious effort to calm down, Raven dialed again. This time she let the phone ring. On the third ring the line opened up. Raven couldn't breathe.

"Hi, this is me. I'm not able to come to the phone right now which means..." A machine? The damn machine picked up! Raven couldn't believe this. How annoying.

".... At any rate leave a message. I'll get back to you."

B-E-E-E-E-P

"Johni? This is Raven. I just wanted to call and..." The phone suddenly picked up.

"Raven?" It was Johni's voice. Oh Lord, Raven thought, she is home. What do I say now?

"Yes," Raven said in a very small voice. "How are you?" Raven couldn't believe how stupid that sounded. Why did she feel so stupid when she opened her mouth around this woman?

"Fine," Johni answered and Raven's heart dropped a bit, "except that I miss you," Johni finished. Raven's heart was now in her throat.

"You miss me? Really?" She asked. A warm feeling started in her toes and was now steadily working its way up her body.

"Of course I do," Johni answered, "Did you think being the beautiful woman that you are you could just shadow in and out of my life in just one day?" Raven was smiling hard. What was this woman saying? God, how bold! She loved it.

"Beautiful? You think that I'm beautiful?" Was all Raven could get out.

"Yes Raven, I think that you are incredible," Johni answered. Damn, Raven thought, she loved how this woman said her name. She made it sound so musical and so important. She didn't care if no one else in the whole world ever said her name again as long as Johni did.

"Thank you," Raven said, "What are you doing?" She had to steer this conversation back into the friendship swing.

"Writing," Johni answered. Raven felt a tug at her heart. She really liked the idea that Johni was a writer. It was so exciting.

"Really? Are you working on anything in particular?" Raven was asking very superficial questions but she didn't know what else to ask. She couldn't ask what she really wanted to.

"A manuscript. It's a horror story."

"Really? I'd like to read it sometime." Raven really meant that.

"Anytime," Johni responded. "When can I see you again?" Raven's heart skipped a beat.

"I don't know. I really just called to see how you were," Raven answered. She knew in her heart that Johni didn't believe that.

"Oh, okay, I'm fine. When can I see you?" Johni asked again. Johni was pushing but Raven didn't feel pushed.

"I really don't know Johni. Maybe soon," Raven answered suddenly feeling really uncomfortable. "Look I have to go but if it's okay I'll call again?" She didn't want to hang up but felt she needed to.

"Of course you can call anytime," Johni said. "Anytime at all."

"Okay, well, I'll let you get back to your writing."

"Bye Raven."

"Good-bye Johni." Raven hung up the phone and it felt as if someone had ripped her heart out and stomped on it. She hadn't wanted to hang up. She wanted to talk to Johni, to ask her all sorts of questions. She wanted to talk to her about yesterday and her feelings, and life in general. She felt so incomplete right now. She felt a strong yearning for Johni. A need to be with her, she felt.... love. Oh Lord, she felt love for her. Olie was right. Raven was in love with Johni. Now what was she going to do. She felt the love swell within her chest as she put a name to the feeling and acknowledged it. Damn! Now what? She had the urge to tell someone what she was feeling. She dialed Johni's number.

"Hello?" Johni's voice answered.

"I think that I'm in love with you." Raven blurted out and then hung up the phone. She felt a mixture of excitement, stupidity and wonder looking at the phone. She couldn't believe what she'd just done.

* * *

Johni just stared at the phone in her hand. Did she hear what she thought she heard? Did she say that she thought she loved her? Johni was dumbfounded. Replacing the phone back in its cradle she walked to the patio and sat down on the steps. Loves me? She said that she loves me? Johni wanted to call her back and make sure that she had heard right but she didn't have the phone number.

After they had parted yesterday Johni came home and sulked. She had meandered around the house and felt as if her attention span had a log time of about 3.2 seconds. She couldn't concentrate on anything at all. She'd tried to write, clean, read, everything but nothing worked. She hadn't felt like this in a very long time. Her heart felt broken. The thought of never holding or even just seeing Raven again was unbearable. She had picked up the phone a number of times to see if Olie had Raven's phone number but had felt, considering the way in which Raven had left, it warranted her not calling. Now she calls, tells her that she thinks she loves her and then just hangs up? The nerve. Johni had to laugh despite herself. A mixture of excitement and fear filled her body. Now she had to call Olie. She had no choice. Picking up the phone Johni took a brow beating but finally got the number from Olie. She sat for a long time considering how this had to be done. What if she were wrong? What if Andi answered? What if Raven had changed her mind? There were so many things to consider. Finally, mustering up the courage to call, Johni dialed Raven's number.

"Hello?" It was Raven. Johni was unsure what to say, she was at a complete loss for words.

"Raven? It's me, Johni." A sharp intake of breath came over the line. "Are you able to talk?"

"Yes," was the answer but Raven offered nothing further. She seemed to be waiting.

"I need to ask you if I heard what I think I heard." A small giggle escaped Raven.

"What do you think you heard?" Raven was toying with her and she could feel it. This was a good sign.

"Did you say that you loved me?" Johni held her breathe waiting for the answer.

"I said that I think I love you," was the response. Johni was perplexed. She wasn't entirely sure what this meant. Suddenly she felt a self-assuredness that she could not place.

"So..." Johni started, "what do we do to make you sure?" Raven laughed. Johni knew that she was coming on strong but for some reason it was okay. She felt safe with the way in which they seemed to be relating. She had never felt so sure about anything in her whole life. She knew that she just had to have this woman.

"How do you know that you can make me sure?" Raven asked. She loved this little game they had started. It was becoming fun for Johni as well.

"Oh I can make you sure," Johni answered. "You just

have to give me a chance." Another small giggle could be heard over the line. Johni smiled.

"You just might get that chance Ms. Andrews," Raven said, and then quickly, "Johni I have to go Andi just pulled up." With that she had hung up the phone leaving Johni holding the other end of the line feeling incomplete. She had to fight the urge to call Raven back and say, "Screw Andi, and marry me." Marry me? Where did that come from? She had to laugh. She had never even considered marriage until this very moment. She hadn't considered it with anyone. (Not after all the crap Brenda had put her through.) Could she do that? Could she marry Raven and be happy? Yes, she decided, she probably could. With that Johni sat down to write Raven a letter.

Andi had pushed re-dial. Raven couldn't believe she had made such a stupid mistake. Now ranting and raving Andi was in Raven's face asking for an explanation. Quite frankly, Raven really didn't have one. What was she supposed to say, sorry honey I fell in love with someone else. Oh this was just so wrong.

"Who is she Raven?" Andi yelled. "Who is this person?" Andi's veins on the sides of her neck started to pop out. It would have been comical if it were not for the killer look in her eyes.

"A friend, Andi." Raven saw no point in making this worse. Hell, she wasn't even sure if Johni was exactly what she wanted. (That wasn't true.) She needed to be sure before taking any steps with Andi right now. "It's just someone Olie introduced me to. A writer. You would like her." Raven knew that she wasn't going to convince Andi but it was worth a try.

"Olie? Damn Raven, you know that she's always trying to fucking fix you up with someone else!" (Raven never understood Andi's excessive need to speak like that.) "What does she think she's doing this time? Finding someone smarter than I am?" (Raven hated it when she started this.) "I'm smart too you know, but no, you think I'm stupid. You and your damn friends and your family." (Well, here we go on the family, just leave the kids out of it.) "Your son and daughter are just so full of themselves! Spoiled, you're all fucking spoiled! (She had to start in on the kids. Andi just didn't know when to quit.) Hell Dionne alone...." Raven had to stop it here.

"Don't go there Andi," Raven said firmly. "You don't want to say anything you'll regret." Andi softened for only a moment.

"Or what? You going to kick my ass, Raven?"

"If I have to," Raven responded. It always ended up here. It was like Andi wasn't happy until there was a physical challenge. Raven hated violence in the worse way. She would never let Andi get the best of her though. Andi shoved her and Raven had to regain her composure before she said anything else. Andi mistook Raven's moment of non-action as weakness.

"You're such a wimp Raven. You couldn't kick my ass if you had an army to back you up." Raven held onto her temper just a little harder. She was feeling the strain. "You and your damn family! Nothing but a bunch of snobs! You all think you're better than everyone else! But you're not, you, your daughter and that mama's boy you call your son!" That was it. She just couldn't hold onto it anymore. Andi had left her no choice.

"You're crazy, you know that? Just like your mother, you're nuts Andi! I see why she cracked up. Look at you! You probably drove her to it!" Raven had gone for the throat. She had chosen the area that she knew would screw with Andi most. Andi's mother was a manic depressant and Raven knew that Andi secretly feared that she too would one day become sick. At this point though she didn't care. Andi's face turned a new shade of red, almost a purple and Raven knew this was going to get physical. Oh well, she thought, there's no turning back now.

"You take that back!" Andi demanded. Raven could not only take it back but now she had a whole bunch to add to it.

"No, because it's true! You better be thankful that your daddy's dead Andi because he would definitely be ashamed of you right now!" Andi jumped on Raven. Raven did all she could do to just fight her off. She could hit Andi but she didn't want to hurt her. Geez, in the middle of this physical assault she was worried about whether or not Andi got hurt. There was something sick in that. Andi hit her two or three times and Raven just blocked all of the blows. Andi finally picked up an ashtray that lay near-by. She held it up as if to strike Raven. Raven was scared but refused to back down.

"That will be the last thing you do!" Raven stated in a low, even tone. Andi knew she wasn't playing. So she lowered the ashtray. For a moment Raven watched in awe as Andi's temper transformed into self-pity. It always happened this way and it always managed to surprise Raven at how easily the transformation took place. Andi started to cry. Oh damn! Raven thought.

"Why are you always so mean to me Raven?" Andi wailed. She always did this. She'd start something and then find a way for it to be Raven's fault. Raven, yet again, resigned herself to the fact that there was just no hope in getting Andi to understand. Raven turned to walk away.

"Who is she Raven?" Andi asked crying a little harder. Raven stopped. More than anything she wanted to turn around and tell Andi that she was in love with someone who was twice the woman she was. Again, however, she chose to protect Andi.

"No one important Andi. Just a friend," It was hurting

her heart to say that but she knew it was necessary.

"Are you leaving me Raven?" Andi asked. It was more a statement than a question. Raven looked into Andi's eyes and mustered up the strength to be a little honest.

"I don't know Andi," Raven said as gently as she could. "If things don't change for us I'll have no choice. I just can't live this way anymore." Andi put her face in her hands and cried even harder. Raven started to reach a hand out to her but it just wouldn't move. Shaking her head, Raven turned, went to the bedroom and locked the door.

Chapter 6

Finishing eight pages in less than twenty-five minutes Johni sat back. She had written so hard that she was starting to sweat. As she reread the work she had just put down on paper she could hardly believe she had written it herself. The scope of emotion within these pages was unbelievable. She read them over three times trying to decide if she were coming on too strong. She was, but that seemed the only way it could be. She was so conscious of the emotion she was feeling in other areas of her life that it was becoming apparent in her written work. It is said that the strongest writing is the work that is accomplished during really emotional times in a writer's life. This definitely qualified as an emotional time in her life, and then some. Setting the pages down on the desk Johni picked up the phone receiver. She held it so hard that her knuckles started to turn white. Putting the phone back down she just sat and stared at the computer screen. She wanted so badly to call Raven. To make sure she was okay. She knew doing so would not be a good idea. "Damn!" She said out loud to the empty house. The sound of her voice hung in the air. The fact that she lived alone was more apparent now than it had ever been. Picking the phone up again Johni dialed Raven's number.

"Hello?" It was Andi. Johni hung up quickly. She had

hoped Raven would have answered. Disappointed Johni stared out the front window. All Johni could do until Raven called her, was wait.

* * *

When the phone rang Raven just let Andi get it. She didn't want to talk to anyone right now anyway, except Johni. She knew with all of Johni's cockiness even she wouldn't go that far. Since Andi hadn't come to the door, Raven figured that it must not have been important. Lying on the bed, Raven thought over her earlier phone conversation with Johni. She smiled. Flirting with Johni had given her sort of a rush. She had felt playful in a sexy way. That was something she hadn't been comfortable enough to do in a very long time. It was really too bad that Andi had interrupted the conversation. Raven was suddenly angry with Andi again. It seemed like all she did these days was get mad at her. No, actually, all she could feel lately for Andi was disgust. Andi thought that Raven didn't know how she was. It wasn't only Andi's dependence that prompted her to consider leaving but her disloyalty as well. She knew that, given the chance, Andi would cheat on her. But could she feel right cheating on Andi? She was actually cheating on Andi in her heart now but all she could do was get mad rather than feel guilty. Shaking her head Raven had to wonder. When did things get so bad? There was a knock at the door.

"Raven?" Andi. Did she ever know when to leave well enough alone?

"What?" Raven didn't move from the bed. She had no intention of letting Andi in here.

"I'm going out. Did you want anything?" Yeah, Raven thought, how about some ice cream and while you're out get a brain and personality transplant for yourself.

"No," Raven answered. For a few moments Andi was silent. Then Raven heard Andi kick the bedroom door and then slam out the front door. After a couple of seconds she heard Andi speed off down the street. Good riddance, Raven thought. She let herself relax now that she was in the house alone. Her mind wandered. She could see herself spending the rest of her life with Johni. In her mind's eye she saw their wedding, where they would live. She could see it all. Quietly Raven started to cry. Her heart ached for Johni. She looked at the phone. She could call her. No, she shouldn't, not with the way she was feeling right now. Getting up off the bed Raven started to pace. But why shouldn't she call? It was just a phone call. Besides it was starting to get dark outside. She hated the dark. The phone rang and Raven practically dove for it.

"Hello?"

"Raven?" It was Andi. Raven felt her heart drop like a rock.

"What Andi?" Raven knew that she sounded annoyed but she couldn't help it.

"I'm not coming home tonight."

"Why Andi?" Raven asked still annoyed. Why must there always be a scene?

"You don't want me there anyway so I'll just stay away." Andi was crying softly. Raven felt a small tug at her heart. Damn, she thought, if I could just harden up, just a little and tell her to fuck off. Andi was quiet on the other end and Raven became suspicious.

"Where are you, Andi?" Raven was becoming aware of the fact that Andi was obviously not alone. Raven thought she could hear another voice in the background.

"I'm at Devin and Tammy's," Andi said defiantly. Raven could not believe this. But then again, yes she could. Of all places to go, Andi chose Raven's son's home. She always tried to involve the kids.

"Andi, don't get Devin involved in this." Even as she said the words she knew that it was no use. Andi used everyone. Raven's son was as kind hearted as she herself was. She knew Devin wouldn't let Andi stay on the streets. There was no telling what Andi had told them.

"Why, Raven? Are you afraid that your kids will find out how you really are?" Andi spat out. Raven could hear her son in the background telling Andi to cool it.

"Good-bye, Andi." Raven hung up the phone. She hated

hanging up on people but she could not help it with Andi. She refused to talk to her when she was being so mean. She understood that Devin had to help Andi, which was the way she and Walker had raised the kids. The thing that really pissed her off was that this was just more ammunition for Tammy. Raven's heart ached when she considered her relationship with her daughter-in-law.

In the beginning, when Devin had first started bringing Tammy around, she had gotten along with everyone. Especially Raven. However, as the years passed the distance within the relationship had grown between her and Tammy. Tammy seemed to be jealous of her. Try as she might Raven just couldn't make sense of the change. There had been no great falling out. One day she had just started noticing how distant Tammy was becoming. When she questioned her son he had no idea what the problem might be. Then, one day, Tammy just blew up. She had yelled all sorts of awful things and in the end Raven ended up defending herself behind things she didn't understand. These days she tried to leave well enough alone so that Devin didn't have to deal with it. Tammy still jumped at any chance to talk about Raven or start a rumor or two. Half expecting Andi to ring back she got up and went to the bathroom. She decided to go to bed early. Pulling back the covers she looked at the empty bed. She hated sleeping alone. Crawling in and pulling the covers up to her chin she tried to get comfortable. She couldn't. She was lonely and more than a bit aroused. Just as she were about to give up the phone rang. Picking it up after the third ring she was sure it was Andi. She wasn't looking forward to another fight, not even on the phone.

"Hello?" Raven said tiredly.

"Did I wake you?" It was Johni. It was as if she had sub-consciously called to her.

"No, not at all." Raven answered trying to contain her excitement.

"What are you doing?" Johni asked. Raven loved her voice. She felt herself even more turned on.

"I just got into bed," Raven said with just a hint of seductiveness in her voice. Johni gave a small quiet laugh and she knew Johni had picked up on it.

"Oh, and what were you thinking about in bed?" Johni didn't know where Andi was right now but she really didn't care either.

"Would you be surprised if I said you?" Raven answered. Johni felt a rise within her body.

"Me?" Johni said softly in the deepest voice she could muster up. "What was I doing?" A soft moan came over the phone.

"Touching me," Raven breathed. Johni held her breath for so long before answering that she had to remind herself to let it out.

"Where?" Johni asked, she was almost begging to be told. Raven put her hands on her breasts.

"My nipples; you're touching my nipples." Raven responded. The heat from between her legs was apparent now and Raven felt her body longing to have Johni really there with her. This, if done right would do for now. Raven had a fleeting thought that she should stop but then she dismissed it.

"Would you like to tell me what I'm doing to your nipples or would you like me to tell you?" Johni asked. Raven moaned quietly.

"Tell me please," she begged. Johni took in a sharp breath and let it go.

"I'm running my tongue over them, first the right and then the left, taunting and teasing them into awareness. Nibbling on each one until they are harder than they have ever been at any other time in your life." Raven moaned again, this time louder.

"Tell me more," Raven said gasping slightly for air. She hadn't been this aroused in a long time. She could not believe that this woman was making love to her over the phone as if she were there in her arms.

"After spending a little time on those nipples I would be able to smell your arousal." Raven felt a sharp familiar pull within her body. Oh my, she thought, I'm going to have an organism while she is talking to me on the phone. Oh

Raven, she thought, this is bad.

"I'm a slow, gentle lover Raven." (She loved the way that Johni said her name.) I would take my time, making sure that I ran my tongue into and through every curve between your legs." Raven's body tightened with pleasure. She couldn't believe what this woman was doing to her.

"Please go on Johni. Would I enjoy it? Would you make me scream?" Raven breathed. She had to finish this. She was on the verge of satisfaction.

"Oh yes, Raven. You see I'd touch your body until you almost had to release and then I'd enter your body searching for that one spot and release your passion and make you cry out with pleasure." Just as Johni finished her sentence Raven felt herself reaching orgasm.

"Oh Johni," She cried out softly.

"Come for me Raven," Johni responded, "Come for me baby." Raven came with all of the force in her that had been pent up for years. She couldn't believe what she was feeling. Wave after wave of pleasure washed over her body as she met organism again and again. Over the phone hearing Johni release only served to enhance her own. The noises that she was hearing over the phone line turned her on more. Johni's groans were low and guttural. After what seemed like several minutes, Raven's body finally started to relax a bit. She could still feel a tingling between her legs that she was sure from this moment forward would never go away. Out of breath and drained Raven searched for something to say to Johni.

"That was wonderful," Raven said quietly. A soft laugh came over the phone.

"It certainly was," Johni responded. She too sounded out of breath. Raven felt sure that she had affected Johni in the same way that Johni had just affected her.

"Was it good to you?" Raven asked in the most incredible after sex voice Johni had ever heard. Johni felt herself start to get aroused again.

"Yes, it was," Johni answered. "Go to sleep now, Raven. I'll talk to you in the morning." Johni hung up. Raven replaced the receiver and laid back. She smiled. She felt more satisfied at this moment than she had ever felt in her life.

Chapter 7

As the sun streamed through a small crack in the bedroom curtain Raven lay in bed wondering what to do next. Andi had come home but she had slept on the couch. That was okay with Raven. After her phone conversation with Johni last night she was sure that if Andi had come to bed she would have somehow given herself away. Thoughts of the phone conversation coursed through her mind and Raven again felt herself aroused. She was experiencing a mixture of pleasure and embarrassment. She smiled despite herself. She couldn't help the way she was feeling. It wasn't just the phone sex but the feeling of total connection between Johni and herself. She had never felt this way before. Looking at the phone, Raven considered calling Johni this morning but quickly shelved the thought opting for a shower. She would never appear too eager. While in the shower, Raven again felt that now familiar rise in the pit of her being. This time however, she did not give in to the urge as before but simply finished her shower with a smile. Toweling off she relived last night's phone conversation. It had been a very long time since anyone had been able to make her feel that good. She reveled in the feelings that she was experiencing. Sitting on the bed Raven again stared at the phone trying to decide if she should call. As if she had willed it the phone rang, startling her. Picking it up quickly Raven was sure that it would be Johni. She was instantly disappointed.

"Hello?"

"Raven?" It was Andi. Raven's heart dropped.

"Yes?" Raven answered. She was not going to get into it with her first thing this morning.

"I'm sorry I left without saying anything but I didn't want to wake you. I figured you were still mad anyway." Andi stopped. Raven knew that she was waiting for Raven's offer of forgiveness. She was not going to give her that though. Raven was tired of being the one to give in. Every time they fought Raven ended up taking the blame. Not this time.

"What do you want, Andi?" Raven asked with the slightest hint of annoyance in her voice. Andi picked it up instantly.

"Did I interrupt you Raven?" Andi spat back. Raven knew that Andi was trying to bait her. She wouldn't bite, not this morning.

"Why no Andi, as a matter of fact I was just sitting here by the phone waiting for you to call." Raven was as sarcastic as she dared to be. She couldn't help it; she was tired of Andi's shit. There was an audible click on the line indicating that Andi had hung up. Raven couldn't help but smile to herself. Just ruined her day, Raven thought as she dressed. At least Andi wasn't here to make it physical. Dressing casually Raven decided to get out of the house. Grabbing her keys, Raven headed for Mac's.

* * *

Johni walked into Mac's and before she could take a seat Olie was by her side. Opening up her newspaper Johni totally ignored Olie and pulled it up to read. Olie swept the paper from her hands.

"Oh no you don't! Give!" Olie said with a smile. Johni toyed with her.

"What do you mean? I don't know what you're talking about." Olie sat down hard in the seat across from Johni.

"Tell me what's going on between you and Raven," She pleaded. Johni had to admit she was having fun watching her beg.

"Raven's got a girlfriend."

"And..." Olie responded. She was getting impatient.

"And, nothing. She's a nice person. We are becoming friends." Johni didn't want to discuss her personal feelings with anyone but she also didn't want to offend Olie.

"Friends? Well, I guess that's okay, for now," Olie said thoughtfully. Johni had to laugh.

"Well, gee, thanks for your permission." Olie looked confused for a second and then joined in the laughter.

"Coffee smart ass?" Olie asked getting up.

"Please," Johni said going back to her paper.

* * *

Raven prayed all the way to Mac's. She had to be there. If nothing else happened all day today Raven had to see Johni, or at the very least talk to her. She couldn't believe that she was feeling this way. She felt like a schoolgirl. The very thought of seeing Johni thrilled her to death. As she pulled into Mac's she wanted to cry out in joy when she saw Johni's Jeep. Pulling into a vacant parking stall it was all Raven could do not to run into Mac's. Getting out of the car and making sure that her hair and clothes were acceptable, Raven regained her composure and, with all the style and grace that had become her personal trademark, Raven walked into Mac's.

Johni was not reading the morning paper. It was in front of her but her eyes could not focus. She was reliving last night. She could still feel her minds hands on Raven. She could hear the sounds Raven had made over the phone line. She couldn't help but adjust a little in her seat now as she remembered the wonderful coupling that had taken place within their minds last night. As good as it felt to have Raven over the phone Johni could only begin to imagine what it will be like to really hold her in her arms.

She had to smile. Johni had already decided that their being together would only be a matter of time.

Raven looked around as she entered Mac's. She knew that people noticed her when she entered a room so she always tried to make it worth their while. She smiled at her own arrogance. Scanning the room Raven nodded to Olie and then found Johni at her regular table. Her heart leaped and then sank just a little. Johni had the damn paper in front of her face. How the hell was a woman supposed to make an entrance for someone if they have a damn newspaper in front of them? There's a habit she'd have to change. Raven made her way across the room and stopped just short of Johni's table. Folding her arms in front of her she cleared her throat.

"How are you supposed to notice the women who come in the door if you've got that paper in your face?"

"Who needs to notice women when you're completely taken with one in particular?" Johni responded lowering the paper slowly.

"Good answer," Raven laughed. "May I join you?" Johni got up and offered Raven a seat.

"Please," Johni answered. Raven sat down and gave Johni her best smile. Her heart pounded so loudly that she feared it might be heard even over the noise of the other patrons. Johni smiled back. Raven had grown very affectionate towards that boyish smile Johni commanded.

"What brings you out so early this morning?" Johni asked conversationally. A million proper answers flooded Raven's mind, however, only one made its way to her voice.

"You."

"How did you sleep?" Johni asked obviously pleased with Raven's first answer.

"Good. You?"

"I did all right but something still seemed to be missing." Johni answered. This small talk was killing Raven. She longed to be in Johni's arms.

"Missing? Lose your Teddy?" Raven asked teasingly.

"Something like that," Johni said smiling. She appeared to be so calm. Raven was a little irritated that Johni seemed to be so collected. She should be on pins and needles like she was. Raven sat forward.

"Are you always so cocky?"

"Shouldn't I be?" Johni asked leaning forward as well.

"Was last night a sample or was that it?" Raven teased. She already knew in her heart that last night was definitely only a sample. She could tell by looking at her that Johni would know how to please a woman.

"A taste," Johni answered, "only a taste." She smiled and Raven noted that her smile was just a little crooked. It was cute. Raven began to feel a little warm so she sat back. She saw that Johni's attention was on something behind her. Turning she saw Olie making her way to the table. Oh no, she thought. Johni must have read her face.

"Tell her nothing and she'll go away." Raven smiled and prepared to greet Olie.

"Girl, you better not come in here and not say hi and give me a hug." Olie said practically lifting Raven from her seat. Raven rose and hugged Olie.

"Hi Olie, how are you today?" Raven asked with a smile. She really liked Olie a lot but she was a busy body. Olie had come to get the 411.

"Fine, fine," Olie answered. "Johni already admitted to nothing so I won't waste my time on you too. What will you have to drink?"

"Coke," Raven answered. "With cherries Olie," Johni chimed in. Raven was again pleasantly surprised. She smiled and told Olie thank you. When Olie was out of earshot she turned to Johni.

"That was sweet. Thank you."

"The lady likes cherries, she should have cherries," Johni responded as if there simply was no other explanation. Raven liked that.

"Do you treat all women like this?"

"Only those who drive MG's," Johni answered.

"You know many women with MG's?" Raven teased.

"Only one," Johni responded matter-of-factly. She smiled at Raven and again she thought that she was going to lose her composure and tell Johni to take her now. Johni, however, appeared to be completely calm. How annoying, Raven thought to herself. She'd never had a woman be so, calm in her presence. Oh you need to quit, she told herself. Olie brought her coke and right away Raven fished out a cherry. Putting the cherry in her mouth she looked up to discover Johni looking at her smiling.

"What?" Raven asked suddenly self-conscious.

"You do like the cherries don't you?" Johni asked.

"Sort of," Raven smiled, "I guess it's more a habit now. My mother use to put them in my cokes."

"Your mother and you were close?"

"Yes," Raven answered, "very close. She's been gone for a while now but I still miss her." Johni nodded. She didn't know why she was getting so personal with Johni. It must be the comfort she felt. For some reason she felt at ease with this woman. As if they'd been friends for a long time. "My mother spoiled me, I guess. She always took care of me in a way that it seemed nothing was too good for her little girl. My brothers are the same way."

"How many brothers do you have?"

"Three. The oldest has passed away but the others stay nearby. They would like you," Raven said with a smile. The guys had never really been too keen on Andi. They would instantly respect Johni, Raven was sure of it.

"I want to see you again," Johni said leaning closer.

The suddenness of her statement caught Raven off guard.

"When," was all Raven could ask? Johni seemed to be studying her face and then she sat back just a little.

"Tonight," Raven's mind raced trying to make it possible. She knew that Andi would be off work at seven. She could set it up so that Andi thought that she was going to Susan's. Raven hated to use her daughter like that but hell...

"Okay, when?" Raven blurted out. She didn't care about anything else but being with Johni.

"Meet me on Reman's at six," Johni answered.

"Okay, I'll be there," Raven, said with a smile. There was an uncomfortable silence between them for a minute or two. An air of conspiracy seemed to hang over the table. Raven looked at her watch.

"I'd better go," she said getting up from the table. Johni stood with her. Such a gentleman, Raven thought.

"I'll see you tonight then, at Reman's?" Johni asked. For the first time since Raven had arrived Johni seemed a little anxious.

"Yes, I'll be there." Raven answered with a smile. Reassured Johni smiled back. Raven walked to the door turning only once to wave good-bye to Johni. She felt good with this woman's eyes on her. She felt safe. It had been a long time since she'd felt this way. Walker had been the only person to make her feel that. He, too, had a way of looking at her that made her feel as if the world would have to go through him first to get to her. Leaving Mac's Raven felt exhilarated at the thought of meeting Johni tonight. She couldn't wait.

* * *

Johni watched Raven leave. Coming or going that woman looked good. She could not remember a time when she had ever felt so strong so quickly about a woman. Tonight. She needed desperately to hold this woman again. If they never did anything else physically, as long as she could hold Raven she would be complete. She really enjoyed the conversations that they had shared thus far. The intelligence that Raven commanded intrigued her. She seemed so sure of herself. The little touch of arrogance that Johni detected was adorable. She liked a woman who knew who she was. Johni finished her coffee and paid Mac. Leaving Mac's Johni felt good. Finally she felt as if she was going in the right direction.

Chapter 8

Andi stomped around the house for nearly an hour without saying anything at all. She was home when Raven returned from Mac's. Raven had no idea that Andi was taking the day off until she walked through the front door and was bombarded with a speech about how inconsiderate she had been. How was she to have known that when Andi had called earlier it was to tell her that she had made special plans for them? Hell she was not a mind reader.

"Raven," Andi said finally, "We need to talk." Raven sighed loudly but let herself be led to the living room. She was not looking forward to this. Andi took things to such extremes. Talking with Andi almost always turned into a confrontation. Raven was wearing thin in the patience department. Sitting down on the couch she readied herself for whatever was to come. Surprisingly, Andi sat down next to her and for a moment dropped her head. She appeared to be considering what to say next. Raven didn't know how to react to this because Andi was being unusually calm.

"Andi, what do you need to discuss?" Raven asked carefully. She didn't want to say the wrong thing. When Andi lifted her head there were tears in her eyes and a look Raven hadn't seen in a long time. She couldn't help but take Andi's hand. Damn her bleeding heart, she thought.

"Raven, I love you with all my heart but I don't know what to do to fix what's wrong with us." Andi meant what she was saying. Raven's heart sank. Oh Andi, she thought, why are you waiting until now to do this? All Raven ever wanted from Andi was to talk, to communicate, and now...now that Raven had found someone else Andi wanted to talk. Why was life so unfair? She felt herself leaning towards giving Andi a chance.

"Andi," Raven began, "for so long I've wanted our relationship to be on solid ground but you were never willing to try. You couldn't have thought that I could spend the rest of my life like this." It was always funny to her how most people go on about their lives never considering that the way they treat the people they love could drive them away.

"I know Raven," Andi answered quietly. I know that it may be too late but I need you to know I am willing to try. Four years is a long time to just throw away. We made a commitment and we have to try to save what we have. Please give me a chance." Raven's mind reeled. What should she do? She loved Andi but she had decided that she couldn't stay with her. What about Johni? She knew somehow in her heart that she and Johni should be together but what of her commitment to Andi. Damn! Why did she have to be so damn committed to her word? Why couldn't she be like everyone else and just let go?

"Andi, how do I know you mean what you're saying?" Raven asked. She knew damn well this was a new thing from Andi. Chances were Andi really did want to try. Andi was reaching.

"I guess you really don't," Andi answered. "I suppose you will just have to trust me. I know you have no reason to but I love you, Raven, and I need you in my life." Andi was pleading and Raven felt like scum. Andi really did love her. Raven knew this to be true. But she just wasn't sure if Andi knew how to love her in the way she needed. Raven resigned herself to make what felt like the hardest decision of her life. Although she was falling in love with someone else, her commitment was with Andi. Since Andi was willing to patch things up, the least she could do was make an effort. After all, she owed Andi that much. She reached out and took Andi into her arms. Andi cried harder. Inside Raven was aching. Aching to be with Johni.

"It's okay Andi," Raven soothed. "We'll try. You're right, four years is a long time to just cast to the wind." Andi cried a little while longer. Finally she pulled back to wipe her eyes. Raven was perplexed. She felt that she had finally gotten through to Andi but somehow it seemed too late. Andi went to the bathroom to clean up leaving Raven alone to contemplate the decision she had just made. What would she tell Johni? I'm sorry, I think I'm falling in love with you but I can't do that now. I have a relationship to mend. It sounded so stupid, but it was true. She had to give herself and Andi one last chance. Johni would surely understand. Tears welled up in Raven's eyes and flowed down her cheeks uncontrollably. Her heart hurt so much. Why was life so unfair?

* * *

Johni came home from Mac's and wrote non-stop for three hours. She took a break and went to the frig for a Michelob. Johni wasn't a big beer drinker but after a good writing session or at the end of the day she really enjoyed one cold beer, sometimes two. It helped to relax her from the emotional high writing put her on. She took the beer to the back porch and sat down. A hummingbird was flitting in and out of the new feeder she had hung last weekend. It was a beautiful sight. Not as beautiful though as her Raven. Her Raven. Johni was already possessive. She smiled to herself. What a woman. How the hell could anyone treat her less than perfect? Johni loved everything about Raven. Her smile, her laugh, the way she tilted her head downward and then slowly look up as if to say, I'm shy but in a very sexy way. There was a whole list of things Johni wanted to spend the rest of her life getting to know about Raven. The softness in her voice, the compassion in her eyes, even the arrogance with which she said things was appealing. Raven expected to be heard and she expected to be loved. Johni liked that. It made life much easier if your other half expected certain things of you. Your other half?

"Gone girl," she said out loud, "completely gone." Johni was ready and willing to give this woman everything and anything she ever wanted. The word "no" would simply not apply to Ms. Michaels. Johni would collect the world for her and set it at her feet.

* * *

As six o'clock approached Raven's stomach began to turn. She was getting physically sick thinking about telling Johni that she had decided to give Andi another try. She was experiencing dread in the worse way. She had already decided to go and meet Johni at Reman's. It was the least she could do. Andi was doing her best to win Raven back. She had been wonderful and attentive all day. She took Raven to lunch and then shopping. Raven's heart wasn't in any of it but Andi had been so beside herself with joy that she hadn't seemed to notice, or maybe she just didn't want to. Raven had mentioned to Andi that she needed to go to Dionne's. Andi hadn't pushed to join her, thank God. Raven promised that she'd only be an hour. Andi said she'd cook dinner for the two of them. At 5:35 p.m. Raven set out for Reman's. For the first time in her life she would be early for something. She smiled bitterly at the thought. I'm going to be early for the ending of my own happiness, she thought. She needed desperately to get this over with.

* * *

Johni had always been a good driver. She prided herself in using her signals and driving the speed limit. Tonight, however, she was driving much faster than she normally would have. She was running ten minutes late and she didn't want Raven to think she wasn't coming. They had done enough of that not showing up on time dance already. Maneuvering the Jeep around first one slow driver and then another, Johni could think of nothing but getting to Raven. When she came to the bottom of Reman's she caught herself singing softly to herself. She smiled as she realized that it was Celine Dion's, "I'm Your Lady."

* * *

Raven parked the MG and got out. She went to the edge of the cliff and looked out over the city. Dark was just beginning to fall and the city lights were slowly creeping over the town. The scene was very reminiscent of how she was feeling inside. The dark was slowly creeping into her soul. Tears once again welled up in her eyes as she thought of the first time she and Johni were here on the Hill. Would she ever get over this woman? She knew that a part of her was dying inside but her sense of commitment wouldn't let her give up on Andi. She had hurt person being in her life in order to do what would make her happy. She wouldn't let it happen again. This time she would think of someone other than herself. She had to be responsible. God how she hated that word...responsible. She walked back and sat down on the hood of the MG. She smiled as she remembered Johni's words to her about the car, about her being the only woman who owned an MG. How was she going to do this? How could she deny what her heart wanted most?

* * *

She sat in the truck just below the turn-off. If the bitch comes up this way she would see her. Andi could see Raven from where she was parked. Look at her! She says she won't leave and then turns around and comes right up here to meet with the bitch.

"I'll be damned," she heard her dead father's voice inside her head, "you just can't trust anyone these days." Andi slammed her fist into the steering wheel.

"Shut-up!" She told the old man's ghost, "Just shut the fuck up." Laughter inside her head mocked her.

"I told you the old bitch would do this. Should've

listened to your old man and killed her way back when..."
Andi squeezed her eyes shut. Why didn't he just leave her
alone? Dead. He was dead and still a pain in her ass. Hell
had she known she would have never taken the pains to
kill him in the first place. She could have gone through this
with him alive. Stabbed him. Stabbed him at least a
hundred times in the mouth and he STILL wouldn't shut up!
Chills ran up her spine. Had too. She had to kill him, he
was hurtin' mom. Made her crazy.... Crazy as a loon... She
barked for Christ's sake. She had to kill him before he
made her crazy too. She opened her eyes again and
watched Raven move towards the edge of the hill.

"You could do it right now," the old man chimed. "Just
travel on over there and kick her prissy ass right off the
hill. Might be fun to watch her bounce off all those rocks."

"Shut...up!" Andi said tightening her grip on the wheel.
She needed to think. She didn't want to kill Raven. She
wanted to kill the writer. She looked at her watch.
6:10pm. The bitch was late. Andi climbed quietly out of
the truck. From her position she could see the road from
the bottom of the hill up. In the distance she spotted a car,
no a truck, maybe, coming towards the hill. That was her.
Andi took another long drink from her fresh beer. Wiping
her mouth on her sleeve, she made a split second decision.
She couldn't wait for the writer-bitch to come to her. She
smiled as she climbed back into the truck. She would meet

her at the curve. She'd meet her there and then shove Johni Andrews, the writer-bitch right off the hill.

* * *

Johni never saw the truck. She was rounding the third curve up the Hill when the truck appeared out of nowhere. In a split second decision Johni braked hard to the left. She heard a loud crunching noise and absently thought, there goes the paint job. As the steering wheel bent into her mid-section Johni thought she heard someone call her name. She never saw the tree.

* * *

At 6:30 p.m. Raven stood alone on the Hill. Johni had made her decision for her. She hadn't come. Raven had prayed hard for God to find a way for her to not have to face Johni. This must have been His answer. It didn't matter why Johni had changed her mind, only that she had. Getting back into the MG she started down the Hill. She fought the tears as they fell softly down her cheeks. She was going to stay with Andi and she was going to make the best of it. Maybe Andi finally had changed. Maybe this was the one thing that made her finally see the light. Taking the fourth turn down the Hill she came upon what looked like an accident scene. Slowing to yield to the police flares, Raven glanced over at the ambulance as they loaded a person on a stretcher into it. She said a small prayer for the victim as she did whenever she happened upon a scene such as this. Poor soul, Raven thought. Someone somewhere is waiting for that person to arrive and they'll never get there. What a shame. Eager to get home to the glass of wine that she was certain would ease her breaking heart, Raven concentrated on the road. She never noticed the tow truck pulling the white Jeep from around a big oak tree.

* * *

The doctors and nurses worked on Johni for nearly eight hours. Finally, they stopped the internal bleeding and got the swelling around her brain under control. Although she was in critical condition, she was stable for now. The hospital contacted Mac and Olie as Johni's next of kin. Although they were not related they were listed on record as her emergency contacts.

"How is she?" Mac asked the doctor who was in charge.

"She's stable but comatose." Olie took in a sharp breath and started to cry. Mac put a comforting arm around her.

"We don't know how long she'll be like this," the doctor continued. "Maybe days, maybe longer. The next twenty-four hours will be crucial. All we can do is wait.

If there's someone else, you may want to contact them. She may not make it at all." Olie and Mac hugged each other. Johni had no family. Her parents had died long ago and she had been an only child. Mac and Olie knew that they were all the family she had.

"I think you should call Raven," Mac said quietly. Olie nodded and went to the phone. She dialed Raven's number, hung up and dialed again. Replacing the receiver she rejoined Mac.

"Well?" Mac asked.

"Number says it's disconnected," Olie said distracted, "I don't know where she lives." Funny, she thought, Raven hadn't mentioned getting the number changed. Mac cleared his throat and it broke her train of thought.

"Well there's nothing else we can do." Mac said, "Hopefully she'll find out and come on her own."

* * *

For two days Raven tried to contact Johni. All she got was the damn machine. She must have left eighteen messages. At this point she didn't give a damn anymore. Obviously Johni didn't really care after all. If she did she would at least call. How could she have been so wrong about her? She was doomed to spend her life with Andi. Andi's "trying" lasted a full twenty-four hours. She'd woken up the morning after they'd had their talk just as mean as ever. She decided during the night that Raven was indeed having an affair and woke up pissed as hell. She even informed Raven, in a fit of rage earlier that morning that she had gone so far as to change their phone number. Raven couldn't believe it but at this point she didn't care. She didn't care about anything anymore. She was in the kitchen doing dishes when she heard Andi click on the TV. The damn thing was so loud but Andi acted as though she were deaf anyway. She was listening to the local news.

"Raven, come watch the news with me," Andi yelled over the TV. It wasn't a request but a demand.

"No," Raven answered coldly. She had given this fiasco with Andi a lot of thought and concluded that she would leave Andi anyway. She couldn't live like this anymore. She would get her own apartment and live alone.

"Come on, you never watch TV with me." Andi whined.

"I said, no. It's too depressing." Raven hated it when Andi whined.

"You ought to think about someone else for a change." Andi yelled out. Yeah, Raven thought, whatever. The newscaster's voice drifted into the kitchen.

"The accident that critically injured a local writer has been ruled a drunk driving incident. Although the accident was a hit and run the State police have surmised that the other driver was drunk and may have actually caused the accident. Alcohol bottles were discovered at the scene and one witness reports seeing the driver of a truck throwing bottles out of the window moments earlier." What a shame Raven thought as she picked up a plate to dry it.

"The injured victim was Johni Andrews, a local writer best known for writing horror books. Andrews has been a local celebrity for more than eight years now and...." As Raven caught the name the plate she'd been holding hit the floor before she could recover. Rushing into the living room, Raven stood in horror as Johni's picture flashed across the screen. Andi looked at Raven as though she'd lost her mind.

"What's your problem?" Andi asked flipping the TV off. Raven lunged for the remote.

"What hospital?" Raven screamed turning the TV back on.

"What?" Andi asked.

"What hospital?!" Raven screamed again not finding the story.

"Mercy," Andi said, watching Raven grab her keys and head for the door. "Raven what the fuck are you... The front door slammed shut.

Chapter 9

"Johni Andrews, where is she?" Raven asked the nurse at the front desk. She realized that she was upset and not being very polite but she couldn't have cared less what this little woman behind the desk thought of her.

"Are you a family member?" Raven didn't have time for this.

"Yes," she smiled tightly, "a distant cousin." The nurse looked skeptical for a moment and then thumbed through a card index file.

"Room 337 in CCU. Third floor."

"Thank you," Raven responded heading for the elevator. The nurse was saying something about family members when Raven pushed the third floor button on the elevator. Family members my ass, she thought as the elevator lifted. She nervously watched the floor numbers climb. Damn, this elevator was slow. What kind of shape would Johni be in? What would she say to her? Oh Lord please let her be all right. Raven had been silently praying all the way here. Praying. She remembered back briefly to that night on the Hill. She had also prayed then. She had prayed that God would make a way for her not to have to face Johni. Tears welled up in her eyes. Her mother's voice cut into her sub-conscious like a knife, "Be careful what you pray for Raven Ann, you might get it."

The elevator door slid open revealing a nurse's station and a quiet corridor beyond. The floor was strangely silent except for the constant drone of machines. She was immediately assaulted with the antiseptic odors associated with hospitals. The smell always made her sick. The entire scene brought back memories of Walker. She choked back tears. Stepping across the threshold Raven heard someone call her name. Olie rushed to Raven from a set of chairs on the left side of the corridor. She hugged her quietly. After a few moments Raven let go and took a step back.

"How did you find out?" Olie asked wiping her eyes. "I tried to call but your number has been changed."

"Andi," Raven said. Olie nodded to indicate that she understood. "I saw the story on the news. How is she?" Olie dropped her head.

"Come sit down Raven." Raven's heart leaped to her throat.

"How is she Olie? Is she all right?" Leading Raven over to the chairs Olie motioned for her to sit and then joined her. Raven's heart felt as though it was going to burst from her chest.

"Olie," She pleaded, "Please." Olie took her hands.

"Raven, she's in a coma." Raven took in a sharp breath.

"A coma?" Tears filled Raven's eyes and threatened to spill over. She did her best to hold them back.

"A drunk driver hit the Jeep and the Jeep hit a tree. She was in surgery for eight hours the night they brought her in. There was some internal bleeding," Olie explained, "but worse than that there was some swelling around her brain. Her head hit the windshield pretty hard." Olie was now crying openly. Raven squeezed her hand "You can't tell by looking at her that it's that bad. She just won't wake up." Olie continued. "Mac and I have been here, in shifts, day and night since it happened. The doctors believe that she can hear us talking to her, telling her to fight." Raven's stomach was in knots.

"When will she wake up?" She knew this was a pointless question, but she had to ask.

"They don't know. They say that some people stay in comas for years."

"Years?" Raven exclaimed, "No." She wept openly now. She wept for herself as much as for Johni. "I want to see her." Olie nodded and got up from her chair. Raven followed quietly. She didn't care if Olie realized how she felt about Johni anymore. She could no longer hide it. Nor did she want to. Olie led her to room two or three doors down the corridor. Raven paused at the door. She needed a moment to prepare herself. All kinds of horrible pictures had entered her mind. Olie waited patiently. Raven finally opened the door and stepped in. The room was full of machines that all appeared to have lines leading into

Johni. At first Raven wasn't sure she could go any further, but the moment she saw Johni she went to the side of the bed. Other than her head being wrapped and a few bruises Johni looked as if she were asleep. Raven reached down and touched her hand lightly. It felt cold, too cold. In the dim light of the hospital room her skin looked pale. It gave Johni a ghostly appearance that made Raven uneasy. She scanned the machines recognizing a heart monitor and breathing machines.

"The doctors tell us to talk to her," Olie whispered. Raven looked at Olie who gave her a weak smile. "I'll wait outside." Raven waited until the door shut and then turned her attention to Johni. Oh God how could this have happened? She rubbed Johni's arm. She searched for any reaction from Johni to her touch. There was none. Bending down she touched Johni's face, caressing her cheek.

"Johni?" Raven said quietly. "It's me, Raven." Tears spilled over Raven's cheeks. "Honey, I'm here. I'm so sorry about Reman's. I was there but when you didn't come... Oh baby...I had no idea. I'm so sorry." Raven's heart ached so badly. She felt like dying herself. There was no reaction in Johni at all. Raven continued to rub her cheek and speak softly.

"You have to get better. You have to come back to me. Please Johni wake up." Raven felt helpless. She cried harder now not caring if anyone came in. Pulling up a chair she sat down beside the bed and wept. She cried hard for several minutes. Fate had played a cruel joke on her. She had been given the opportunity to see Andi for who she really was and now the very person who could take care of her and make her happy was here, lying close to death. Finally exhausted from crying she sat and held Johni's hand telling her that she had to get better. She begged, pleaded and even got angry, but it was no use. Johni still did not move. Raven sat with her for two hours before Olie finally came in.

"Raven?" Olie said quietly. "Come on, let's go get some coffee." Raven looked up at Olie and blinked. Leave? Was Olie asking her to leave Johni's side?

"What if she wakes up and I'm not here? I don't want her to wake up and be alone." Olie reached out and helped her up.

"It'll be okay Raven, if she wakes up the nurse will call us." Raven nodded. She leaned over and kissed Johni on the forehead.

"I'll be back honey," she whispered softly in Johni's ear. "I love you." Raven let Olie lead her from the room. She felt like a zombie as Olie took her downstairs to the cafeteria. They sat and drank their coffee as Olie tried to convince Raven to eat something but Raven just refused. After a couple of quiet moments Raven broke the silence.

"This was my fault."

"What?" Olie asked surprised. "What do you mean your fault? She was hit by a drunk driver."

"She was coming to see me!" Raven answered, tears re-appearing. "We were supposed to meet on top of the Hill." Olie nodded. Raven had taken the opportunity while sitting at Johni's side to convince herself that if it weren't for her Johni wouldn't be here.

"Raven, you had no way of knowing." Olie took her hand and squeezed it. Raven couldn't remember a time when she had felt so helpless. They sat in silence for a while.

"Does Andi know?" Olie finally asked. Andi. Raven had forgotten all about her.

"Who cares?" Raven answered coldly. Had she not fallen for Andi's bullshit again maybe she wouldn't have been praying and maybe...Oh, hell, maybe nothing! If Johni wasn't okay nothing would ever be right again. Her life would be empty. As if she had heard her name Andi appeared in the doorway of the cafeteria. Spotting Raven and Olie she walked straight to them. Raven couldn't believe the nerve.

"What the hell are you doing here?" Andi demanded. She cut right to the chase. That was Andi though; Raven thought to herself, no manners what so ever.

"I'm here to see a friend," Raven answered coldly. She hoped Andi would pick up on it and leave. No such luck.

"Friend? What friend?" Andi was pissed and Raven was pretty sure that she had put a lot of it together. "Who is it Raven?"

"Excuse me, Raven, I'm going to check on things," Olie said getting up from the table. "Hello to you too, Andi." Andi sniffed at Olie and then took her seat across from Raven. Lord please make her go away, Raven prayed silently.

"None of your damn business!" Raven was about to lose her composure.

"Who is this woman Raven? And what is she to you?" Andi persisted. This was a conversation that Raven just didn't want to have right now but she supposed she had no choice. She readied herself and spoke slowly to answer Andi's questions.

"She's a very close friend. She was in an accident several days ago. I just found out today and I needed to be here for her," Raven said evenly. Andi looked dangerously controlled.

"Was it the writer in the news story this morning?"

"Yes."

"Is this the woman you went to the play with?"

"Yes," Raven answered watching for a reaction in Andi. She saw nothing but control. This was new and frightening. Andi took a moment before asking her next question.

"Are you in love with her?" Raven took a moment to answer. She figured what the hell; things couldn't possibly get any worse.

"Yes." Andi's face turned beet red. Raven was afraid for a moment that she might be having some sort of attack. It looked almost comical. Andi suddenly got up and stood above her. Raven was sure Andi was going to hit her. Instead, Andi lifted the table between them and shoved it to the side. Oh my God, Raven thought, she's lost her mind. Getting up quickly, Raven moved a couple of steps away from Andi who was standing, fists balled up, breathing very hard. Raven couldn't help but think of how ridiculous Andi looked.

"Andi! Have you lost your mind?!" Raven asked. "What are you doing?!" Andi started to shake.

"What am I doing?!" She screamed. "What the fuck are you doing?!" Several people had gathered at the door. Raven was sure that someone would call security. She hoped they would anyway.

"Andi calm down," Raven said quietly. Andi took a step towards her and Raven readied herself.

"Don't do anything you'll regret Andi," She warned. Andi stopped for a moment.

"Regret?! Regret?! I regret ever becoming involved with a selfish bitch like you! I can't believe you're cheating on me! What the fuck can this woman do for you that I can't?!" Andi screamed. Raven glanced at the people in the doorway. Several of them were whispering. Oh great, she thought; now we will be the topic of discussion for the rest of the week. She could hear it now, "Hey did you hear about those two lesbians...."

"Andi this isn't going to help anything," Raven said trying to calm her down. "Why don't we talk about this later, at home?" Andi lunged for Raven catching her by the hair. Raven swung at her trying to break free. Just as she felt Andi let go two security guards grabbed Andi from behind. She swung wildly at them both. It took them a couple of minutes but finally they got her under control and in handcuffs. Helping her to her feet, they both held on tightly. Incredibly, Andi was still trying to fight them.

"Are you okay?" One of them asked Raven. Straightening her clothes and hair Raven said yes, she was fine. For the first time she smelled alcohol on Andi.

"Bitch!" Andi screamed, "I'm going to make your life hell. I'll kill you! I hope your girlfriend dies and if she doesn't I'll kill her myself!" Raven couldn't take it anymore she reached out and slapped Andi across the face. The action caught everyone off guard, especially Andi.

"She hit me!" Andi yelled. "You let her hit me and I'm handcuffed!" Andi started to cry loudly. All Raven wanted was to be away from here. Olie rushed back into the room and grabbed Raven.

"What the hell..." Olie said looking at Andi.

"She's lost her little mind!" Raven said coldly. "Whole fucking family is nuts!"

"I'll kill you! I'll kill you bitch!" Andi screamed.

"Get her out of here!" One of the security guards said to Olie.

"Gladly!" Olie answered leading Raven from the room. Once outside, Raven broke down and cried. Olie held her for some time. Finally, Raven was able to stop. She felt spent.

"How could I ever have been with her?" She asked out loud more to herself than to Olie. She was realizing just what kind of person Andi was. How could she have lived with her all this time and not know that Andi was capable of this?

"It doesn't matter now honey. All that matters is that it's over," Olie soothed.

"How's Johni?" Raven asked hopefully. Olie shook her head.

"There's no change honey." Raven dropped her head. She knew that she and Andi were definitely a thing of the past. She was suddenly relieved. It would just make things less complicated. She knew as she watched the newscast this morning that her heart was with Johni and with Johni was where she intended to be. She felt complete with

Johni. In her heart she realized that a life without Johni would be no life at all. For now all she had to concern herself with was Johni's recovery. Suddenly, an unpleasant thought occurred to her. What if Johni had somehow known that she had changed her mind that night? What if she had somehow realized that Raven was meeting her to sever any ties they had?

What if, when she woke up, Johni didn't feel the same, or worse, what if Johni died?

Chapter 10

Raven was at the hospital day and night. She had Olie go to the house for clothes and little things that she knew she would need. Andi had put up a fuss but eventually gave in and let her take Raven's things. Raven knew that she would have to face Andi sooner or later. Today, exactly one week since Andi had made a complete fool of herself in the hospital; Raven had decided to get it over with. She would face off with Andi, come what may.

"Are you sure you want to do this?" Olie asked as Raven gathered up her things. Olie and Mac had been nice enough to let her stay at their place. Neither of them were excited at the prospect of Raven going back to the house alone. Raven stopped what she was doing and hugged Olie.

"No. But I need closure. Really, I'll be okay," Raven assured her friend. Olie looked at Mac and he threw his hands up. Raven finished packing her things. She smiled secretly to herself. She knew that her friends meant well but she needed to do this. Mac helped her put her things into the car and Raven set out for home.

Home. Was it home anymore? If she were really honest with herself, she just didn't know. If Andi refused to leave she had already decided to go ahead and move herself. But if Andi decided to leave, would Raven be able to remain there? Turning the corner Raven noticed Andi's truck in the driveway. She really hoped this would go smoothly. For a moment she considered whether she had made a mistake not bringing anyone with her? It was too late now. Parking the MG Raven went into the house.

* * *

There was a smell, sort of antiseptic in nature. Johni opened her eyes. She lay still letting them focus on the ceiling. She could hear a constant beep from her left. She was lying in a bed, but where? Concentrating, she tried to remember what had happened. There was a truck. It had come out of nowhere. She was in a hospital. There had been an accident and now she was in a hospital. A hospital?! She couldn't be here she had to meet Raven! Johni tried to sit up. Pain coursed through her body and she was forced to lay back. Involuntarily, she cried out in pain. The beeping from her left increased. Within seconds of her failed attempt to sit up two nurses were by her side.

"Well, look who's awake," one of the women said with a warm smile. Both nurses looked eerily alike. Johni always wondered if there was some nurse factory somewhere. Where do all of these women who look alike come from? Is it some requirement that they all bear the same description? Who knew? Despite the pain Johni smiled. Both nurses smiled back not realizing the thoughts going through Johni's mind.

"And how do we feel?" One nurse asked. Johni hated these questions.

"Well," Johni said in barely a whisper, "You look fine, I can't seem to move very well." The nurses laughed.

"That's not surprising considering...."

"Considering what?" Johni asked suddenly concerned. Was she missing parts? What?

"We'll let your doctor speak with you." The other nurse smiled. They both left Johni alone in the room. She was full of questions. She felt six years old again. Memories of doctors who would whisk her parents from the room when she had a cold or the flu leaving her young mind to consider death or worse. After all, if it were something small why did everyone have to leave the room? Johni smiled again. It was amusing what your mind carried with it into adulthood. Johni looked around the room now for the first time. There were loads of machines. She recognized a few. The constant beep was a heart monitor. She wondered just how bad the accident was. Where was Raven? Did she know that she was here? Surely someone would have told her? Johni searched her mind again for details of the night of the accident. She was alone, of that she was sure. There was something trying to surface through to her consciousness; some detail that needed immediate attention. The harder she tried to remember the deeper it buried itself. Well, Johni thought, when you need to remember, it will come. The door to the room opened and Olie stuck her head in.

"Hey girl! It's about time!" Olie said rushing to the bedside. Johni couldn't remember being so glad to see someone. She reached up and took Olie's hand.

"Boy, am I glad to see you. These people won't tell me anything and I can't remember a lot," Johni said. "Fill me in." Olie smiled and took a deep breath.

"You were in an accident, a car accident." Olie started. Johni sighed loudly.

"Thank you for stating the obvious."

"Well, I figured I'd start from the beginning," Olie answered. "Do you remember going to meet Raven?"

"Yes. We were supposed to meet on Reman's," Johni answered, her heartbeat increasing at the mention of Raven's name.

"You never made it," Olie said bowing her head for a moment giving reverence to the memory of that night. "It was awful," She went on, "You had head injuries and you went through eight hours of surgery. They didn't think you were going to make it." Johni tried desperately to remember something, she just couldn't.

"You've been in a coma." Olie added.

"A coma?" Johni said surprised. Then a thought crept into her mind, a memory of comas and people. "How long?"

"Since you came in," Olie answered. Johni closed her eyes. A coma? She'd been asleep since she came in? She could have been a coma for a while. She was happier to be awake than she had ever been in her life.

Questions flooded her mind. Was she okay? Was there anything missing? Did all of her parts work? Slowly she started moving her feet and then her legs, working her way up. When she got to her hips she started to feel better. So far so good. She thought to herself. Olie saw what she was doing but didn't have the heart to stop her. Both arms okay. When she got to her hands, Johni realized that she could move the left one very well. Panic started to set in. She looked up at Olie. Her head was down and Johni could see tears.

"Olie?" Johni asked. "Olie what's wrong with me?" Olie squeezed Johni's hand. Johni made a mental note of how good that felt.

"It was crushed in the accident Johni," Olie answered quietly.

"Crushed? What do you mean crushed?" Olie didn't respond and Johni's panic worsened.

"Olie?" She pleaded. Olie was about to say something when the room door opened and a man in a white coat entered.

"Well I see that you are indeed awake," the man said

approaching the bed. Ross was on his name badge. He introduced himself as Dr. Peter Ross.

"What's wrong with my hand?" Johni demanded. The doctor's smile turned into a mask of seriousness.

"Do you have any feeling in it at all?" Dr. Ross asked quietly. For the first time Johni turned her attention to what she felt in her left hand. A little. She felt very little. Involuntarily tears welled up in her eyes. Angrily she swiped them away.

"A little," she answered in a whisper. The doctor went about the business of checking the rest of Johni out. As he did she noted which parts hurt the worse and what exactly was in working order, all seemed in order except her left hand. After completing his examination Dr. Ross did that annoying "doctor thing" and stopped to take the time to write in her chart. Why do doctors always make you ask?

"Well?" Johni asked slightly annoyed. She needed answers. Now. The doctor cleared his throat. Not a good sign, Johni thought.

"Johni, during the crash your left hand was pinned between the outside of your vehicle and the oak tree that you came in contact with. Your hand took quite a beating." Johni looked down at the blanket where she remembered her left hand to be.

"How long will it take to heal?" She asked. The look on the doctor's face told her she shouldn't have.

"It probably won't completely." The doctor answered. "We estimate that you may, at best, recover eighty-five percent use of that hand." Johni's heart sank. Her hand? She was a writer for God's sake. Hell, she was left-handed. Damn! She thought.

"When you're feeling up to it, Ms. Andrews, the police would like to speak to you," Dr. Ross started.

"Johni, please," she interceded.

"Okay, Johni. The police have been by at least once a day the entire time you've been here. I think it would be advisable for you to speak to them. They are driving my staff crazy." Johni eyeballed the doctor.

"What do they want?" She asked cautiously. For the first time since the doctor had come in Johni noted that Olie was still in the room. She was quiet but looked distressed.

"Your accident appears to have been a little more than an accident." Johni was surprised. Not an accident? Who would run her into a tree on purpose? The doctor continued, "The police seem to feel that you may have an enemy or two." Johni couldn't believe what she was hearing as she lay there trying to absorb the information.

"You were in pretty bad shape when they brought you in Johni. Based on the injuries you suffered it would be a little hard to believe that it was just an accident."

The doctor smiled weakly to reassure her and left.

Johni's mind was still racing. Someone wanted to hurt me? Maybe kill me?! Olie sat down next to the bed and took Johni's hand. They were both quiet for a long time. Neither knowing what to say to the other. Finally, Johni broke the silence.

"Who could it have been? Do the police have any leads?" She asked quietly. What she really wanted to ask was if Raven knew, but she didn't.

"Not anything that they have shared with us," Olie answered.

"Nothing?"

"No. Raven has been here but we weren't sure if you would want her to know so we didn't say anything," Olie answered. "It was really hard not to tell her. She cares for you a great deal, but she seems to have enough to worry about." Johni sank into silence. She felt isolated, alone.

"Don't tell her yet," Johni finally said quietly. Olie just nodded. "I need to know what's going on first. Johni lay back deep in thought. She needed to know if Raven was in any danger by being around her. You heard about nut cases targeting writer's all the time. Not exactly what she needed in her life right now, a nut case. Besides she couldn't even use her left hand now. She wondered if the nut would be disappointed that the writer he was chasing was no longer able to write. Karmic justice. Johni smiled bitterly at the thought.

"What are you thinking?" Olie asked concerned. Johni reached over and patted Olie's hand.

"Nothing," she said in a faraway voice, "Nothing important.

* * *

The smell of booze hit Raven like a ton of bricks as soon as she entered the house. It was eerily quiet and dark. All of the curtains had been drawn. The atmosphere was that of a dungeon. Raven entered cautiously not knowing what to expect. As she rounded the corner to the living room the first sight that struck her was all of the bottles strewn everywhere. The floor looked like the final resting place for dead booze bottles. There had to be twenty or so sitting all over her tables and on the fireplace. Anger started to seep into her consciousness. She tried to control it. She had already promised herself that no matter what she would not get angry. But on her furniture?

Making her way through the living room Raven headed for the bedroom. It was her guess that Andi was passed out there. As she approached she heard voices. Voices? Andi wouldn't, her mind protested. As she reached the door however she was positive there were at least two voices coming from inside. Slightly opening the door, Raven peered in. There, in her bed with Andi, was none other than Raven's friend Lee. Andi was on top of Lee oblivious to any other presence. Raven went into shock. She and Lee had shared a seven-year friendship. She couldn't believe Lee would do this. She decided to leave without saying anything. The whole scene embarrassed Raven. Backing up she accidentally hit the hallway table knocking off the books. The noise caught Andi and Lee's attention.

"What was that?" Andi asked as she jumped, getting off of Lee. Raven wanted to run but knew she wouldn't be able to make the door before they caught her. In a matter of seconds she made her decision. Moving forward she burst through the door.

"What the hell is going on here?!" She shouted. Andi stopped dead in her tracks. Lee looked like an animal caught in a trap. Neither knew what to say. Raven had the upper hand just the way she preferred it.

"Andi? What the fuck are you doing?" Raven asked again. Andi looked stricken and then her expression hardened. Oh God, Raven thought to herself, she doesn't even care that she's been caught. Lee got up, dressed quickly, and then made for the door. When she got to Raven she stopped and smiled.

"I told you she was no good," Lee said quietly. "Now maybe you'll admit that now." That said Lee left. After a few moments Raven heard the front door close. She shook Lee from her mind and turned her attention to Andi.

"What do you have to say?" Raven asked sarcastically. Andi fell back onto the bed and propped up on her elbows.

"What do you want me to say? That she was good? She was. One of the best fucks I've ever had," she smiled. "You dumped me and I needed some good pussy." Raven felt rage welling up inside her.

"Lee?! You needed Lee?!" Raven shouted. "Andi, come on. This is low even for you." Raven stomped out of the room. In the living room she busied herself picking up the bottles. She wanted to turn around and throw every one of them at Andi. Andi had followed her and was standing in the hallway entrance. Raven was determined that Andi speak first.

"You dumped me," Andi said casually as if she had done nothing wrong. Raven was not going for the you-did-it-to-me crap.

"Andi I NEVER slept with Johni. I haven't had the chance!"

"That's just like you to be self-righteous!" Andi shouted. Here she goes, Raven thought. "You can be wrong but I can't. You're a worthless bitch!" Raven couldn't take it any longer. Something came over her and she turned on Andi. Before she knew what she was doing she had Andi on the floor and her hands on her throat.

"You listen to me you little Bitch! I want you out of my

house and out of my life right now. If you ever come near me again..." Andi's eyes were as big as silver dollars but quickly narrowed. Raven had to admit, as much as violence appalled her, that this was kind of fun. Andi was really surprised but gained her composure quickly.

"You're going to want to get off me now," Andi stated calmly, "before I rip your heart out."

After a few unsure moments Raven straightened up and got off her. She couldn't believe the ton in her eyes was getting increasingly wilder. Raven could see that she was struggling to keep it together. Suddenly, as Raven expected, Andi lost it.

"You're crazy!" Andi spat out. "My mother and sisters were right! You're nuts!" Raven turned slowly and smiled at Andi.

"You're the one who's crazy Andi. Just like your mama." Andi started forward but the look in Raven's eyes must have stopped her. Instead Andi turned and went back to the bedroom. A few moments later she re-emerged with two large bags.

"I'm leaving." She announced as if Raven should care.

"Bye," Raven responded continuing to clean up. Andi started towards the door but then stopped and set her bags down. She turned and walked back to where Raven was cleaning. Raven didn't look up but continued to busy herself as if Andi weren't standing there.

"You know Raven, you shouldn't mess with people the way you do. You never know what a person might do." Raven continued to ignore Andi until she finally turned and left. After Raven heard the truck start and pull out of the driveway, she finally relaxed enough to cry. She cried for a long time. She cried for her dead relationship with Andi, for Lee's final betrayal, for herself and for the hurt Andi and Lee had heaped on her. Finally she got up and straightened her clothes. She had to move on now. Johni was in the hospital and she was Raven's first concern. She had to get this place cleaned up so that when Johni woke up Raven could bring her here and take care of her.

Chapter 11

A killer. Of the millions of things Johni ever considered dying from, murder hadn't been one of them. Although she had lost her parents at an early age, she had always been self-sufficient and felt fairly safe. She couldn't recall one person, within her lineage, that being the victim of a violent crime. Her parents had died what she considered a violent death but it was a plane crash. The idea that she could have her very own stalker was unnerving.

At Johni's request, Olie had left to give Johni some time to think. Think? Think about what? Hiding? She didn't want to think, she just wanted it all to go away. It just hung there, in the air right above her like a dark menacing cloud. Her basic instincts were taking over. She was now reluctantly weighing her options. Needless to say, a part of her kicked and screamed the entire time, trying to force her back under the covers where the outside world would appear to have gone away. The responsible side of her, the side that her mother had so deeply seeded, won out. Picking up the nurses call box Johni pressed the button. She figured that she might as well talk to the police and get that over with. The desk nurse answered instantly. Johni had to smile, she was sure she had scared all of the floor nurses into submission.

"What can I do for you, Johni?"

"I guess you can let the cops in here next time they show up," Johni answered. The nurse smiled.

"Great, because Officer Collins is here now." She left quickly before Johni could stop her. A couple of seconds later a tall dark harried man entered her room. He looked to be of Italian descent with the typical nose and dark bushy hair. His eyes were foreboding but set into a kind face. It was as if his face and eyes were contradicted each other.

"Ms. Andrews, I'm Detective Art Collins of the Seattle Police department. I have a few questions to ask you if you feel up to it." The voice coming from Detective Collins served to match the inconsistency. It had an unusual pitch, almost high enough to have been mistaken for a female with a husky voice.

"Sit down Detective," Johni smiled. "I'll help in any way I can."

"I understand your doctor filled you in somewhat."

"Not really. All he said was that you'd want to talk to me because you suspected that the accident may not have been an accident at all."

"That's true. There are a few things to indicate that you may have been intentionally run off the road," Collins answered. "We're still investigating."

"I don't have any enemies, Detective." Johni was uncomfortable with the idea that someone might have it in for her.

"It may not be someone you know. You are what we consider a celebrity and in this day and age there are all kinds of nuts that stalk famous people roaming around," the detective offered. "What do you remember about that night?" Johni thought about it for the first time since she woke up. She tried to remember anything that she thought might help. She drew a blank.

"I don't remember anything strange."

"Don't try to remember any one thing," Collins suggested. "Just tell me exactly what happened, say an hour before you started up that hill." Johni thought about it.

"Well... I was meeting a friend at the top of the hill and I was supposed to be there at six but I was running a little late," Johni started.

"Why were you late and by how much?" Collins interrupted. Johni lay there trying to think. Why had she been late?

"I had taken a shower and got dressed...uh I went to the Jeep and..... the tire!" Johni exclaimed. "My front left tire was flat. I had to take the time to change it."

"Great! Now what happened once you got to the Hill?" Collins pushed.

"I started up the hill. Music was playing on the radio and I was absorbed in my thoughts..."

* * *

Celine Dion's Power of Love, such a beautiful song. Wonder if Raven likes it too. I'll have to mention it to her. Damn, this mirror is always crooked. I have got to get that fixed. It really is a nice night. It's a great evening to be meeting Raven. What will she be wearing? How will she look? What will she...tires screeching, headlights...Oh God they are headed right for me....got..to..get..off..the..road...

"...I remember putting my arm out the window to fix the side mirror. All of the sudden there were headlights in my face. I remember trying to pull off the road to avoid whoever it was. Then everything went completely black. Next thing I remember is waking up here." The detective was writing. When he finished he turned back to Johni.

"Are you sure that's it? You don't remember anything else? What the other car looked like, a sound, anything?" Johni thought about it. She tried until her brain hurt.

"No, nothing." Collins closed his notepad.

"Well, I thank you for your cooperation. Like I said, right now we are investigating. I'll let you know what we find. In the meantime you should watch things going on around you for a while. There may still be a chance that this was just a drunk driver though." Collins stood up.

"You don't think so do you detective?" Johni asked carefully. Collins hooked his thumbs in his pockets and favored Johni with a serious look.

"Off the record?" Collins asked. Johni nodded. "I think someone hit you on purpose. Whether or not it was a crazed fan, whoever did it aimed for you." A shiver ran up Johni's spine.

"Any ideas, Detective?"

"Well what we do know is that the vehicle that hit you was fitted for a bra. There were no paint chipping but there were torn pieces of vinyl," the detective explained. "We also know that the skid marks don't match those of an accident. It appears to show that the other car swerved intentionally to hit you. There had to be quite a bit of damage to the other car. Whoever did it will have to get their vehicle fixed so we are checking garages. Other than that all I can say is we are working on it."

"I appreciate that," Johni told the detective. "I'd see you out but well, I can't." Collins smiled half-heartedly.

"No problem, you owe me one," he joked. Johni was beginning to like this cop. "We'll have an officer posted outside your door until you're released. Then, if you'll let us know where you'll be, we can offer you some protection until the investigation is closed." Johni smiled.

"Thanks Detective but I think I'll be okay."

"Here's my card," Collins said handing Johni a business card. "Call if you think of anything." Johni accepted the card with a nod. As Collins turned to leave something slipped out of Johni's sub-conscious.

"Detective, I do remember something." Collins turned back to her.

"What?"

"Rock music," Johni answered.

"Excuse me?" Collins asked.

"Just before the other car hit me I remember hearing ZZ Top. Isn't that crazy?" Johni laughed nervously. Collins whipped out his notebook again.

"Do you listen to that?" He asked writing in the book.

"Hell no! I mean, no I don't. I think the stuff is noise," Johni answered. Collins smiled.

"For what it's worth, I do too. Well, thanks Johni. I'll be in touch." Collins left and Johni lay there thinking. She just couldn't get behind the idea that someone might want her dead.

Raven finished cleaning the house about 1:00pm. She was gathering her things to go back to the hospital when the doorbell rang. Looking through the peephole she saw a man she didn't recognize.

"Who is it?" Raven asked through the door.

"Dave. Is Andi here?" Great Raven thought; what now.

"No, she isn't. Can I take a message?"

"Sure. Can you tell her that this is my bill and ask her to pay it as soon as possible," the man answered. An envelope came through the bottom of the door. "I did some work for her and I just need to get paid." Raven picked up the envelope.

"Okay, I'll tell her as soon as I see her," Raven called back.

"Thanks," the man answered. Raven heard a car door shut and an engine start. She glanced out the window in time to see the man leave. She looked down at the envelope and had the urge to tear it up. All of the problems they were having and Andi was still spending money. In all of the time they had spent together Andi had spent a great deal of money on repair services. She couldn't remember one time when Andi fixed anything herself. Thinking twice about destroying the bill, Raven instead laid it down on the entryway table. She went into the kitchen and called Olie. She got the machine. Olie must still be at the hospital. Picking up her keys from the counter Raven headed back to the hospital.

* * *

"Do you understand what I'm telling you, Johni?" Dr. Ross was talking to her as though she was a child. She hated that.

"Yes," Johni answered. The doctor shifted slightly on his feet. Johni could tell that he was getting a little impatient with her. She didn't give a shit, he didn't have a crushed hand, and what the hell did he know.

"The physical therapy will have to be three days a

week. It's a painful procedure but a necessary one. We have to get you working that hand so you can get the strength back. Your chances of using that hand again are damn good," Dr. Ross continued. Chances. She could believe that her life was now reduced to chances.

"Will it heal completely?" Johni asked not expecting a positive answer. The doctor took a deep breath.

"If you take care of yourself there's a good chance that it will. There are many people who regain full use. You'll have to work at it. That includes mentally and emotionally." Johni looked at Dr. Ross and she couldn't help but note how angry she felt. He was there but he really had no idea what she was going through. There was no way he could understand.

"Will it EVER heal completely?" She had asked this question four times now one more won't hurt.

"Maybe Johni, maybe not."

"Will it always hurt?"

"It could."

"What's the point then?"

"You have to decide that," Dr. Ross answered. "When you do, let me know." With that he left the room. Johni looked up at the ceiling. She was being a brat and she knew it. Throwing a god damn temper tantrum. The nurse had turned off the heart monitor earlier. It appeared that she was out of the woods now. What the hell did they know?

Johni tried to shift in the bed but the pain in her left arm was excruciating. Her arm. Hell she was a writer. She tried to move her fingers. At first she felt nothing but slowly as she started to concentrate she could feel them move slightly. Great, she thought, I'll probably get the use back enough to finger my damn self. Again she felt the tears well up. Damn! She fought them back and again concentrated on what to do next. The therapy was a must if she wanted any chance at all. (There was that word again.) Her arm shouldn't even be an issue. Johni had to know it would be okay. She should be thankful to be alive. She was use to struggling but this was a different breed of trouble. Dr. Ross had said the therapy would be painful but she had a high threshold for pain so that didn't worry her. It was that word chance. If someone could just give her a guarantee that she could beat this she would feel much better. The idea of having to live with only one hand scared her. Johni reached over and pushed the call button. A nurse appeared instantly. Johni wondered if they were prompt all of the time or if she had just scared the hell out of all of them. She smiled slightly to herself.

"Yes, Ms. Andrews."

"Could you tell Dr. Ross that I'm ready to talk now?" Johni asked as nicely as she could. The nurse seemed to relax a little.

"Yes ma'am'," she answered and left. Moments later Dr. Ross appeared.

"You've decided you want your hand back, Johni?" He asked. Johni nodded. "Good. We will schedule your first therapy session for later today."

"Today," Johni asked, "So soon?"

"Well, yes," Dr. Ross answered. "The sooner we get therapy started, the better. Is there anyone we should call?"

"Call," Johni asked?

"Yes, family members or such?" Johni thought for a moment.

"Olie and Mac I guess. Why would I need family members?" Johni asked suddenly unsure again. Dr. Ross pulled up a chair. Oh no, Johni thought, this is not a good sign. Not at all.

"Johni, I have explained that the therapy is painful. Many patients find it easier to weather if they have family support. Are Mac and Olie the only ones you'd like notified?" Johni guessed that the doctor wanted to notify her parents.

"My parents are dead Doctor and anyone else of blood relation is too distant to care."

"I was thinking more along the lines of that nice young lady who has been here from the beginning. Raven," the doctor answered. Raven! Johni hadn't thought about Raven since she first woke up. So much had been happening. My God, what was she going to tell Raven? She wasn't going to want a cripple. She couldn't let Raven see her like this.

"Doctor, if I don't get the use of my hand back, what will my life be like?" Johni asked.

"You should be able to live a normal life with some adjustments."

"There could be problems with the hand in the future though, right?"

"Yes, there could. In fact within the first couple of weeks it will be difficult but after that we should have some idea of how much use you'll regain. I suspect you'll have to go through two or three years of therapy before it's completely useable." Johni had to weigh her options. She didn't want to be a burden to Raven.

"How long will the first session be?" Johni asked. At first she hadn't wanted to know but now she needed to know what she faced.

"Twelve weeks." Dr. Ross answered.

"After that?"

"You'll probably have a short break but then we'll know more about your chances." (There was that word again.)

"So.... by then you'll know if I'll regain use or not." It was more a statement then a question.

"Yes," Dr. Ross answered. Johni took all of this into

consideration. If she could just make it through the first session she would feel better about her and Raven. What would she tell her now though? She couldn't let her know what was really happening. Raven would be burdened herself with her before realizing it. Besides, Johni couldn't even take care of Raven right now and she was with someone who could.

"Don't say anything to Raven," Johni told Dr. Ross. "I'll take care of that. I don't want her to know until I'm able to offer her some hope."

"Okay, but I think you're making a mistake. If you don't mind my saying so Johni, even if you don't regain all the use in that hand you should be able to live a fully functional life."

"If I am it's my mistake Doctor if it's all the same to you." Johni answered. Dr. Ross got up to leave.

"What do you want us to tell her when she comes back?" He asked hesitating at the door.

"Tell her I don't want to see anyone," Johni answered. The doctor nodded and left. Johni lay there listening to the silence. She hoped Raven would understand. She just didn't want to hurt her.

Chapter 12

"What do you mean she doesn't want to see anyone? Tell her it's me!" Raven was livid. Battling the traffic, a flat tire, and a parking space in the middle of nowhere, she had finally arrived at the hospital only to discover this excuse for a nurse at Johni's door.

"I'm sorry but the doctor left instructions that no one is to disturb Ms. Andrews," the nurse repeated. Raven couldn't believe what she was hearing. First this woman tells her that Johni is finally awake and then she tells her that she can't see her. Raven, in the words she'd heard her nephew speak, was about ready to, "throw down."

"I am not leaving this hospital until I see Ms. Andrews," Raven said in the most controlled voice she could muster. "If she doesn't want to see me she'll have to tell me herself!" The nurse was getting frustrated and now she was glancing around for help. Raven was sure she had surmised that if she left the door Raven would not hesitate to go into the room. Perplexed, the nurse pleaded with Raven.

"Miss, if I let you in it could cost me my job. Surely you understand that." The tone in the nurses' voice was a bit condescending. A bit more, that is, than Raven was in the mood for right now.

"Tell me something," Raven said to the nurse, "are you

married?"

"Yes," the nurse answered looking a little confused.

"And if that were your man in there, could anyone keep you out?"

"No." This woman was dense. Raven thought that surely by now she'd get it but it seemed that Raven would have to spell it out.

"I am a lesbian. So for all intents and purposes my "man" is in that room. Do you understand?" The nurse took a couple of steps back as if Raven had just told her that she had rabies. "So if you think your skinny ass is going to keep me from her you have another thing coming. NOW MOVE!" The nurse moved out of the way and Raven barged into the room. Johni looked up, surprised.

"I'm sorry, Ms. Andrews, she insisted," the nurse was explaining. Raven turned and shot the nurse a dirty look. The nurse flinched slightly and left the room. Raven supposed that she would go hide in a closet somewhere and cry now. She didn't care; she needed to think about Johni right now. She turned to look at her. She looked alert and awake but tired. She went to the side of the bed and hugged Johni as gently as she could.

"Hi. How do you feel?" Raven asked quietly as if the scene with the nurse had never taken place. Johni was surprised but pleased; suddenly everything that she had decided earlier was in question.

"I'm okay," she lied. Raven saw right through it.

"Okay now the truth."

"Like I've been hit by a truck." Johni smiled.

"You were," Raven said kissing Johni lightly on the forehead. "But you're okay now so we just need to concentrate on getting you out of here." Johni looked away from Raven.

"It's going to be a while Raven," Johni started. She explained what the doctor had said about her hand. When she was finished Raven could tell that Johni was waiting for a reaction. On purpose she was quiet for a minute.

"Well I guess it's a good thing you write on a computer huh? We'll just have to make sure you do the exercises and make the best of it." Johni was obviously surprised at Raven's reaction. Raven knew she would be. She was aware that she wasn't like everyone else.

"But.... it doesn't bother you?" Johni asked perplexed. Raven laughed.

"What's to be bothered by? I'm sure you can more than make up for any loss of that hand with other things," Raven said with a wink. She wanted to make Johni as comfortable as possible with the injury of her hand. She needed her to know that she was about more than that. Johni smiled at Raven.

"Oh you can bet on that." Although Johni was smiling her eyes still looked haunted.

"What else?" Raven asked matter of fact. Johni was again caught off guard but Raven watched as she quickly recovered and then lost herself in thought. Raven waited patiently.

Johni had to rethink this. She hadn't expected Raven to be so supportive about her hand. Johni wondered if Raven would be so quick to stand behind her when she found out about the "accident". Most people wouldn't be. Johni had been surprised when Raven had barged into the room with an upset nurse in tow. Hell, between the two of them this hospital wasn't going to want to see another lesbian for a long time. Johni looked up and studied Raven's face. She was so beautiful. Johni loved her as much now as she ever had. One of the reasons why she hadn't wanted to see Raven was because she knew it would provoke these feelings. Johni decided she would tell Raven based on her answers to some tough questions.

"What about you and Andi?" Johni asked and Raven sat down. Raven explained the scene at the hospital the first day she had come. She told Johni that at first she thought Johni had changed her mind. But then, she had found out what actually happened and she came right away. She went on to explain what she had walked in on at her home that morning. Johni felt bad for her and wanted desperately to hold her.

"I'm okay though, really. This has been a long time

coming." Raven assured her. Although Johni knew she was hurt she believed Raven. Now, Johni thought, for the big question.

"Raven, will you marry me?" Raven blinked at Johni. She couldn't believe she heard what she thought she'd heard. Johni was smiling at her.

"Are you sure?" Raven asked. She wanted to make sure that Johni hadn't hit her head in the accident or anything.

"Never more sure of anything in my life," Johni answered. "But before you answer there's something we must talk about." Johni suddenly became very serious. Please don't let it be that she kills people or something else I can't live with, Raven thought.

"Okay," Raven adjusted in her chair. Johni took a deep breath.

"The night of the accident something happened." Johni paused only for a moment. "They found out something that might change things for us." Oh my God, Raven thought, she has AIDS.

"What?" Raven whispered.

"Hit and run. They tell me I may have been hit on purpose," There, Johni thought, I told her. Now I'll just wait for the thanks but no thanks. Johni closed her eyes. After a moment she felt Raven hugging her. She held on for a few moments. Johni started to cry. She couldn't help it. She was about to lose the one person in her life that she truly loved. Raven pulled back only slightly and kissed Johni's cheek.

"It's okay; I know you're probably scared. We'll be okay. The police will catch whoever it was." Johni couldn't believe what she was hearing. Did she say we? "I love you Johni. I'll do whatever I can to keep you safe." Johni was floored. She was positive Raven would run screaming from the hospital.

"You mean you want to stick it out?" Johni asked. Raven straightened up and started laughing.

"What did you think I was going to do? Run screaming from the building? If some nut is after you then he's after me too. Besides maybe it was hit and run because who ever hit you didn't want to be caught for the accident." Johni was a little embarrassed that she hadn't actually thought of that. Johni wanted to burst out with I love you. Raven stood smiling at her.

"Is there anything else?" Raven asked.

"Would it make a difference?" Johni answered.

"No, not really."

"Well then, marry me," Johni said.

"Was that a question?" Raven asked.

"Huh? Oh, will you marry me?" Johni asked quietly.

"Yes, I will." Raven answered. Leaning down Raven hugged Johni. They held each other for a while. When Raven finally let go she had questions.

"I want to talk to the police."

"They're here all the time," Johni answered. "They wanted to talk to me the whole time I was out."

"I also want to talk to your doctor."

"He'll be here anytime. They want to start therapy today."

"Today?" Raven asked surprised. "Why so soon?"

"The sooner the better." Dr. Ross answered from behind her. Raven turned around. "We need to get at it before it gets worse." Dr. Ross stepped forward and shook Raven's hand.

"I'm glad she told you." The doctor offered.

"Me too," Raven said with a smile.

"We need to get this started right now Johni," Dr. Ross said addressing her. "I'll explain everything to Raven while you're in therapy."

"Okay," Johni answered as the orderlies came into the room for her. Raven squeezed her hand.

"I'll be right here when you get back," Raven whispered in her ear. She kissed her on the forehead and watched as they wheeled her out. Once she was gone Raven turned to the doctor.

"What now?" Raven asked.

"Well, I'll give you some literature on the therapy," Dr. Ross answered. "Physical therapy affects people in different ways. It can be helpful in some situations depending on a person's physical make up."

"Will it be very painful for her?"

"Yes it will. She has to learn to make those muscles do what they've always done before," Dr. Ross answered. "Watching people go through physical therapy always makes me thankful that I have never had to deal with that kind of injury. It appears to be a very difficult thing to endure." Raven nodded her head. It didn't matter what Johni had to endure, she'd be there. She sat down and settled in to wait.

Chapter 13

At first the physical therapy was painful but bearable but they sat her in a chair and that felt good for a change. However, there was no way anyone could have prepared her for it. The therapist smiled and talked about a lot of insignificant things while removing the bandage from her arm. That was the first clue. Even the therapist didn't want to come clean on what this was going to be like. Johni tried, in vain, to ask a few questions but all she got was an impromptu dance routine. After a short time Dr. Ross came in and took a chair beside her. Her IV stand, with the readout machine ticking away, stood next to the chair. They were taking her off it later today. She looked down as the therapist removed the last of the bandages. Her hand was swollen and bruised. She was suddenly very uncomfortable. Dr. Ross checked the IV in her arm and addressed her directly.

"There really is no way to prepare you for this Johni," He said. "Everyone is a little different. The therapy will be only as good as the work you personally put into it," The look on the doctor's face told Johni that he meant what he was saying. No getting out of this one.

"Meaning," Johni asked? She really just wanted confirmation of her thoughts.

"Whatever the effect it's always painful in some way,"

He answered. Johni sat back and sighed.

"Okay, ready when you are." Dr. Ross reached over and squeezed Johni's good hand. The therapist handed Johni a Walkman and then took the same hand the doctor had squeezed softly working the fingers one at a time. Johni looked at her inquisitively. That one wasn't hurting.

"It helps with the pain," she explained. "Loosens things up." Johni nodded taking the woman's word for it. The therapist traded places with Dr. Ross.

"This is Tracy, Johni. She's going to sit in while you have your first treatment," Johni smiled at Tracy as the therapist took her good hand again. "I'll do it this time then Tracy will from then on," Ross explained.

"If at any time you want to squeeze my hand or if you need anything, I'll be here," Tracy said. "The first time is always the hardest." Johni's discomfort suddenly became fear.

"I don't suppose you could do this for me," Johni asked with a strained smile? Tracy laughed softly.

"No, I'm afraid not." Johni put the headphones on and turned on the player.

"All right then, let's get this over with." The doctor started working Johni's hand. The pain was bad but she was determined not to cry out. The music helped. It was soothing. Johni looked at the clock, four on the nose. The treatment was only supposed to take a half hour. At first she felt a cold sensation running up her arm and it felt good to have someone gently move the fingers but as the doctor worked harder the pain increased. This isn't so bad, she thought to herself. Then, just as she relaxed a little, pain racked her hand and arm. It was coursing right up her arm into her neck. Ripping the headphones off Johni tried to sit up.

"Shit!" She yelled out. Tracy was on her feet as she held on to Johni's other hand.

"It's okay Johni. I know it's uncomfortable but you have to bear with it." Johni looked at the woman thinking, this chick had lost her damn mind.

"It is not," Johni, said carefully, "uncomfortable. It fucking hurts!" The pain localized and became a burning. She wanted to scream but her inhibitions kept her from it. Tracy, as if reading her mind, held onto her hand tighter. Dr. Ross worked the hand in a repetitive motion. The crazy thought that she might actually break the therapist's hand trailed through her mind. Stealing a glance from within her pain at Tracy, however, revealed that, whatever the pressure, Tracy was up for it. The pain didn't stop. In fact it didn't even subside. It was excruciating and constant. Crazy thoughts ran through Johni's mind. First she wanted to rip Dr. Ross's head off. Then a noise started within the room, no in her head. A loud hum that slowly became a roar. She couldn't stop it, couldn't shut it out.

She felt as though the pain was driving her out of her mind. She looked at the clock. 4:08. Eight minutes? Only eight minutes? Johni thought through the roar in her head.

"I can't do this!" Johni yelled at the doctor. "Stop it!" Tracy squeezed her hand harder.

"Johni, listen to me, focus," She was putting the headphones back on Johni's ears. "You have to concentrate on something other than the pain," Headphones? Music? Now?

"Are you crazy?!" Johni screamed. She knew that she was screaming and in the back of her mind she heard a voice saying, what are you doing? You never scream at people. This lady didn't do anything to you. The pain, however, was so constant and so intense that the little voice diminished into nothing. "I CAN'T DO THIS!" She yelled at the doctor.

"You can and you will, Johni," It was not a request it was a statement. Johni felt as if she would lose what little sanity she possessed at any moment now. The burning in her arm became so intense that she was sure her body was on fire. It hurt so bad she couldn't help but cry. She felt as though she was being tortured. 4:15, fifteen minutes to go. She couldn't do this. She was going to lose her mind, she was sure of it. Tracy patiently held her hand as she talked to her but Johni couldn't hear her for the roar in her head. The pain was so intense that she ripped her other hand free and grabbed up the Walkman throwing it as hard as she could at the door. Tracy didn't so much as look surprised. She merely took hold of Johni's hand again and talked to her quietly. 4:18, oh God, Johni thought, please stop. I'm tired I can't do this anymore. She tried to give up. She tried to will herself dead. It didn't work...the pain continued. She tried to make a deal with God. She promised him everything. Still...the pain continued. She cursed and pleaded. Still.... the pain continued. 4:23. Johni tried yet again to get up. Tracy calmly and firmly held her down.

"Johni, you don't have long to go. Hang in there. Focus."

"Fuck you!"

"Focus Johni. Look through the pain and focus," Tracy crooned.

"Fuck you.!" Die. All she wanted to do was die. She didn't care if the hand healed anymore. Screw it. She'd live with it. Anything was better than this. I'm going to be crazy when this is over, she thought to herself. Loony as a bird. A new sensation was working its way into her body. She was sick to her stomach. Not flu sick but pain sick. She heaved and was suddenly glad she had forgone lunch. Tracy calmly picked up a plastic sick dish and held it up for her.

"The sickness you're beginning to feel is par for the

course," Tracy offered. Johni looked at her wild-eyed. She couldn't think straight. She was almost positive that if it weren't for the pain she would kill this woman right now. 4:29, one more minute. Johni watched the second hand on the clock tick off the last seconds. As the second hand rounded the 12 Dr. Ross let go of her hand. The pain didn't stop. She didn't know why she thought that it would. Pain still coursed through her arm. She felt as though she couldn't breathe.

"Still hurts," Johni breathed out gasping for air.

"It's going to Johni," Tracy responded. "It'll be a little while before it stops," As Dr. Ross stood thoughts of his demise filled Johni's head.

"How are we doing?" He asked taking Johni's other hand. We? She thought, what the fuck does he mean we?

"You're trying to kill me," Johni said trying to control her voice. She thought in the back of her mind, however, that she might still be screaming. Dr. Ross looked at Tracy and then back at Johni. It was a conspiracy, Johni thought crazily. They are trying to kill me.

"Johni listen to me. You are going to feel a lot of different things in the coming months," (Months? Did he say months?") "Hang in there; it will subside after a bit. But you must focus on something other than the pain."

"Fuck focusing! I don't want to do this again." Johni said finally calming.

"We can give you pain killers but that's not going to help your hand," Johni glared at the doctor. He was unmoved.

"You can go back to your room. We'll give you a little something for the pain in about an hour," With that Dr. Ross left. An hour? She couldn't wait an hour. She tried to beg Tracy to give her something now. Tracy just smiled and squeezed her hand a little harder. Johni's emotions ran rampant. She was angry, sad, hurt, scared. Her heart couldn't settle on any one emotion. Her muscles burned, her stomach heaved. She just knew that her mind would be the next to go.

"Raven," Johni said to Tracy. "I want to see Raven."

"That's not possible right now. You have to wait a little bit. We need to make sure you don't have any effects from the doctor manipulating your injury," she responded.

Johni lay back and cried. She was going crazy. She would never get through this again let alone for the next few months. Dying could not possibly be as bad as this. Raven. She wanted to see Raven. She needed her. God the pain in her hand was almost unbearable.

* * *

She was screaming. Must be a little painful. It had taken Andi several minutes of sweet talk and lies to find out where Andrews was and now standing just outside the therapy room hearing Andrews scream was worth all the trouble. She smiled. Andrews thought she was going through pain now. Boy was she in for a surprise. People ought to be careful who they fuck. Might get fucked back. Yes indeedy. Fucked, fucked, fucked. A nurse walked by and favored Andi with a suspicious glance. She had snagged a doctor's coat but she knew that her lanky body would look out of place in the oversized garment. She decided that standing here longer was a luxury she could not afford right now. She would have loved to stand there and listen to Andrews scream some more but she had things to do and she didn't need Miss Nosey-Nurse coming back to ask questions. She glided back towards the elevator and as soon as the doors opened dashed in and stabbed the first floor button. She shed the coat and dropped it to the floor. The elevator stopped on the second floor and a cute little redheaded nurse boarded. She smiled at Andi who smiled back and then frowned as she saw the coat on the floor.

"Doctors!" the redhead said, "they are slobs." She bent down to pick up the coat and as she did Andi envisioned herself grabbing the redhead by the back of the neck and slamming her into the wall. Andi shoved her hand into her pocket searching for her pocket knife. She briefly entertained the idea of shoving the blade up into the back of the redhead's neck just to see how long it would take her to die but then the doors opened to the first floor. Shaken from her fantasy Andi nodded her good-byes to the nurse and exited the elevator. She smiled to herself. That redheaded bitch don't know how close she had just come to doing the dance with old Mr. Reaper himself. Making for the door Andi nodded to the hospital security guard. The guard nodded back.

* * *

The waiting was unbearable. Raven spent the first ten minutes sitting in Johni's empty hospital room. It took very little time for that to get depressing. She needed to move around, feel useful. On the other hand she wanted to be here when they brought Johni back. So she walked the hall. The nurses nodded and smiled. Raven guessed they all knew that she was there as Johni's girlfriend. She was sure by now that they all knew she and Johni were lesbians. Raven watched the clock. The nurses had said the therapy would take half an hour and then there would be a half hour recovery time. Recovery from what she didn't know. She wasn't completely sure what all the therapy involved. She made a mental note to ask Dr. Ross if she could go in with Johni next time. As if he heard her thoughts Dr. Ross appeared in the elevator.

"Raven, do you have a minute to come to my office?" The doctor asked. He was very serious and this set warning bells off for Raven.

"Is everything okay? Is Johni all right?"

"Yes, she's doing as well as can be expected," the doctor answered.

"As expected?" Raven asked. "What do you mean, "As expected?" Fear was welling up inside her and Raven felt helpless in stopping it. The doctor sighed.

"Could you come with me Raven?"

"Yes," she answered and followed him to his office. He indicated that she sit as he sat in the chair opposite her. Raven could hardly wait for the doctor to speak. Her mind ran in eighty different directions.

"First of all," he started, "Johni is doing well. She has finished her first session and now we are just giving her some time to get oriented." A thought suddenly occurred to Raven.

"I don't want her to come back to the room and find me gone," Raven said.

"It's okay she won't. I have to see her before they take her back to her room. Raven I need to somehow prepare you for what Johni is going through. Not ever having gone through the therapy myself, it's very difficult to explain what Johni's experiencing. All that I can do is explain what happens and you must take it from there." The doctor stopped to let her absorb this. She had the creep feeling that she really didn't want to know what Johni was having to face. Part of her wanted to know but part of her was afraid to know. She looked up and nodded to the doctor to indicate that she understood so far.

"The therapy will help her regain the use of muscles that have been nearly destroyed," he continued. "These exercises would be nothing for a person without injuries. The fact that Johni's hand is damaged to such a great extent it's going to be quite a painful road back for her."

"So she will be exercising those injured parts of her hand in the same way during each session?" Raven asked. She really needed to understand so she could help.

"Every time. Unfortunately each session will be extremely painful for a while." The doctor was quiet for a moment. "She has to rebuild the tissue and bone as well." Alarms went off in Raven's mind.

"Tissue?" She asked. "What does that mean for her? Will she ever regain full use?"

"It depends on Johni. The harder she's willing to work the more she will get out of it. Patients usually have a difficult time staying with the program. Johni conceivably might have a few problems in this area."

"How can I help her?" Raven asked not sure if she really wanted the answer.

"There are a few ways you can help. I'll give you some booklets that will show you some exercises you can have her do at home. It also suggests some foods that will help in healing. The thing to remember, however, is that it will be very painful. She's strong but she's also been stricken where it will hurt her most. Writing is her craft. I suspect you'll need to work on her self-esteem. She will get difficult and maybe even spiteful, especially after sessions. But it will be the pain talking." Raven smiled a little. "You don't know me very well doctor. I handle everything well. I can be a tough woman."

"What will this do to the rest of her body?" Raven asked quietly. She already had a guess. She knew enough about physical therapy to know it was going to make her sore.

"She will ache a lot. She may even have trouble sleeping at night. It will probably be hard to live with her on session days because the therapy makes her bones hurt at the core. She'll also experience hot and cold sweats. Some nights she won't be able to get warm or cool, these sweats are directly caused by the stresses she'll go through." Raven bowed her head. There was so much for Johni to deal with.

"At times," Dr. Ross continued, "the pain will seem unbearable. She will lose weight during sessions and she will have a hard time eating at all. I won't give her pain pills unless I absolutely have to"

"How the hell is she supposed to handle this?" Raven asked her anger rising. She wasn't mad at the doctor but at the injury.

"Raven, she simply has no choice if she wants to use that hand again." Raven's mind reeled. She had to help. Take some of the pain from her. Something.

"How long does she have to be in therapy?" She asked.

"Sixteen weeks." Dr. Ross wasn't pulling any punches. Raven liked that. She needed to know what they were up against. Sixteen weeks is such a long time, Raven thought to herself. "We have to push the healing. If this doesn't work she'll have to live with her injuries. None of us wants that," he added.

"What are her chances of regaining full use of her hand?" Raven asked, unable to remember ever knowing anyone who'd been injured this badly.

"Unfortunately, at this stage of the game, we don't know. She can go on to healing completely but it'll take a lot of work," the doctor answered. Raven felt helpless.

"After she gets out of the hospital, there are things you can do to help her, the right foods, a good frame of mind, proper ongoing therapy. I'll give you literature on all these things," the doctor offered. "Other than that you need to be prepared for the pain she's going through now. After a while she'll learn to quit fighting and focus on other things. Until then she may get to be a little impossible."

"That's okay," Raven answered. "I can handle it. I love her."

Chapter 14

One week into the therapy found Raven back on Reman's Hill praying to God. The sessions were hard. Raven didn't know what to do to make it better. She had spent so much time at the hospital that she had practically become a staff member. The extensive treatments weren't allowing Johni the luxury of thinking of the two of them right now let alone tomorrow. She was in pain most of the time and when she wasn't she was asleep from the painkillers. Raven realized that Johni was experiencing a lot of depression. Raven herself joined a support group at the hospital. It had become difficult to sleep and she could feel herself wearing thin. She needed to talk to someone before that happened. The support group helped.

Today, standing on Reman's, Raven cried. She struggled to avoid doing so in front of Johni. She refused to show her anything but rock solid support. Although inside there were times when Raven literally fell apart inside. The thought that Johni may never use her hand again was killing her. Raven was doing everything she could to understand. Writing was her career and she couldn't see giving it up but she didn't see things in the same way Johni did. In her mind this was hard but not unbearable. After all in an age with computers and all, the use of only one hand was an obstacle easily overcame.

Still, Johni continued to take a bleak outlook. No matter how Raven felt personally, she had to respect Johni's feelings. She needed to be patient she needed to pray. Reman's, being the highest point in town, might make her feel a little closer to God. Raven got down on her knees to pray. It didn't matter if anyone came along and saw her. The one person she loved most on this earth was in pain and she couldn't do anything about it. She felt no shame in coming here now to ask God to help her Johni. Surely anyone would understand, but if they didn't, screw them. On her knees Raven prayed for Johni. She asked God to take away the pain and make it okay. She asked for his guidance in the things that she would do and say in the coming days. She asked for patience. After she was done she felt remarkably better. She thanked God for easing her mind. She stayed on her knees just a minute longer; enjoying the closeness to God she was feeling.

"What are you praying for Raven? Forgiveness for being such a bitch!" Raven turned to find Andi leaning up against her car.

"What do you want, Andi?" She didn't want a scene. She needed to get back to the hospital. Andi backed up and sat down hard on the hood of the MG. Raven winced but said nothing.

"Want? What do I want? Now there's the question of the hour. What do I want?" Andi glared at her and it was making Raven uncomfortable.

"Andi I don't have time for this..." Raven started. Andi jumped off the car and took a step forward.

"You'll take the time, bitch! No one tosses aside me and just walks away. No one." The tone in her voice put Raven on her guard. She glanced around nervously wishing for a passing car.

"Do we have to do this?" Raven asked as calmly as she could. "I would really rather not fight with you." Andi smiled. It was a crooked smile that made her look crazy. Maybe she's finally lost it, Raven thought.

"No," Andi said walking back to her truck. For the first time she noticed Andi's truck parked a short distance away. She must have coasted in for me to not hear her, Raven thought, what's she up to. "We don't ever have to do this. There are always other options." Raven took Andi's walking away as a chance to make it to her car. But as she stepped forward Andi swung around. "Come back to me Raven."

"No. I love Johni," Raven answered. Andi looked stricken for a moment but then hardened quickly. She opened her truck door and put one foot in. Looking up at Raven she smiled that same crooked smile.

"Die then," she said and got into her truck, gunned the engine and left. A chill ran down Raven's spine. She quickly got into her own vehicle and started back to the hospital.

On the way down the Hill Raven slowed as she reached the sight of the accident. Now, after a month, you couldn't tell there had been an accident here except for the tree that Johni's Jeep had hit. The tree was still standing but the impact had taken quite a chunk out of one side. Raven pulled off the road and walked over to the tree. She reached out a hand and gently ran her fingers over the point of impact. A small shock ran through her body as she realized that this tree could have taken Johni's life. This tree is where this whole mess started. She looked over the area. The tree had served one purpose. It had stopped Johni's Jeep from continuing over the side of the Hill. Just to the other side of the tree was a thirty-foot drop almost straight down. Discovering this made Raven view the tree slightly different than she had just minutes ago. God had been at work here after all, not that she had doubted it before. She made a mental note to point this out to Johni. Raven turned to leave when she felt a sudden pang of anger. She stood on the road facing the direction that she knew the other vehicle had come from. How could someone drink and drive, let alone hit someone on purpose. What an irresponsible act. What kind of a person could do that that? Hell, Raven thought to herself, lots of people do. In fact it was something Andi could have done. Andi. Raven couldn't believe her. She wondered briefly if she were all right. She had been doing things and saying things that were real off the wall lately. She hadn't run into Andi a lot since they had split. Normally she would have undoubtedly run into her a lot by now but she had spent so much time at the hospital that she hadn't had time to go anywhere Andi was likely to be. She was glad. After this last scene with Andi she really could stand to never see her again. Raven crossed the road and got into her car. She sat there for a while considering how a certain moment in time at this very spot had changed her life forever. It was really something the way things worked. Raven headed back to the hospital.

When Raven walked into Johni's room she was shocked to discover her sitting up in bed smiling. Johni had lost a considerable amount of weight but she had otherwise weathered well. The dark circles that showed her physical state were gone. She had also managed to strengthen the rest of her body while working on her arm and hand. Right now the smile on her face did her a world of justice.

"Hey you," Johni said holding her hand out for Raven. Raven rushed forward thanking God for answering her prayers even if only for the moment. They embraced and Raven noted that although Johni was still weak she had gained a little more strength. They held each other for a long while savoring the moment as if it might be their last.

Finally Raven pulled away to get a good look at Johni.

"How do you feel?" She asked sitting down on the side of the bed. She held Johni's hand. Johni smiled again. Raven's heart melted and she ached to make love to her.

"I feel pretty well considering. The doctor came in earlier. He wants to talk to us together so he'll be back." Alarms went off in the back of Raven's mind. Seeing her concern, Johni continued. "He assured me it was nothing bad. In fact he said it was good news." Raven let out a long sigh. (Or was it the breath she had been holding?)

"Where have you been this morning anyway?" Johni asked. Raven smiled. It was amazing how they just sort of fell into this relationship. It was as if they had always been together.

"I went to Reman's," Raven answered, "to pray. You'll never guess who I ran into." Johni waited. "Andi. She was really nasty." Johni straightened up a little. Raven smiled, thinking, my protector. "Down Hero, she didn't try anything. She just ran her mouth. Asked me to come back to her." Raven let her last statement hang in the air.

"And you told her?" Johni fished. Raven smiled.

"I told her I was in love with you." She said snuggling into Johni again.

Johni nodded her approval.

"I can't wait to get out of here," Johni said looking longingly at the window. Her doing so reminded Raven of a question she had been mulling over.

"When you do get out," Raven started carefully, "will you come home with me?" She didn't want to hear it if Johni said no. Instead Johni smiled at her.

"Or go home and take care of myself? As if there is a choice." Johni laughed. Raven swiped at her. Her laughter sounded good.

"That's not supposed to be the only reason."

"Oh baby, you know it's not," Johni soothed. Raven hugged her. She couldn't remember having been as happy as she was at this moment. The door opened behind them and they both turned to see Dr. Ross enter the room.

"Well, we're feeling better I see," he said addressing Johni.

"Yes, I am," Johni, answered. Raven got up and the doctor went about the business of checking Johni, after a time he wrote in her chart and then pulled up a chair. Johni and Raven looked at each other and then the doctor. They were both on pins and needles.

"Relax ladies," Dr. Ross started, "it's not bad. Johni you have quite a bit of therapy left but I think you've gotten to the point where you can handle it. The worse is over now that your body is somewhat accustomed to the therapy. It will still be difficult and somewhat painful but not to the degree that it has been."

"Can I leave?" Johni asked eagerly. It sounded as if that

might be the case to Raven also.

"Yes, I believe you can leave the hospital," the doctor answered. "You'll have a therapy schedule to follow and you can't miss even one session. I think you're going to do just fine Johni." Raven squeezed Johni's hand.

"I'll see that she gets here," Raven told the doctor. He nodded with a smile.

"Your hand is healing fine."

"When can I leave?" The doctor considered for a moment.

"Tomorrow. I want to keep you over just one more night to see how you sleep."

"I can live with that," Johni answered with a smile.

"Good," Dr. Ross said. "Oh and one more thing, your sessions have been cut to twice a week. Do you think you can handle that?" Johni looked surprised. Raven again thanked the Lord.

"I think I can handle that, yes," Johni answered.

"Good," the doctor smiled. "I'll check in on you later." With that he left Johni and Raven alone. For a long time neither of them said a word. They just absorbed the information the doctor had just given them. Raven sat down on the bed again.

"I love you," she said looking into Johni's eyes. They were a beautiful bright green right now and Raven just wanted to hold onto her for dear life.

"I love you too," Johni responded. She took Raven's hand and pulled her up next to her on the bed. For the first time since the accident, they shared a long involved kiss. Fireworks went off in Raven. She hadn't felt this way in a long time. She could feel herself falling deeper in love the longer their kiss lasted. Finally they pulled a part.

"Wow," Johni said quietly. Raven smiled.

"You do have a way with words," Raven said and they both laughed.

"Everything's going to be all right now isn't it?" Raven asked. Just as Johni was about to answer, the door opened. They both turned to see who it was. A woman Raven did not recognize stood in the doorway. She was nice looking. She looked to be about 5'6 with blond hair, maybe in her late twenties, early thirties. She wasn't a nurse, of that Raven was sure.

"Hi Johni," The woman at the door said. Raven turned to look at Johni who looked stricken.

"What are you doing here?" Johni breathed. Raven looked back at the woman and then at Johni again.

"Who is this?" Raven asked Johni. Johni was just glaring at the woman in the doorway.

"Raven, this is Brenda," Johni said in a low controlled voice. The woman stepped forward and extended her hand to Raven.

"Hi," The woman said with smile that Raven didn't

like. "I'm Johni's wife."

Chapter 15

"Your what?" Raven asked staring at Johni. Johni looked disgusted.

"Wife," The woman in the doorway said.

"Ex-wife," Johni spat out.

"Wife, as in, 'until death do us part' and all that mess." The woman now entered the room just as bold as she pleased. Raven took an instant disliking to her.

"What are you doing here, Brenda?" Johni asked tiredly. Brenda just smiled.

"Why, checking on you my love," she answered. Raven noticed a condescending nature about this woman.

"I don't need you to check on me," Johni said. "Now leave." Brenda laughed and took a chair. The nerve, Raven thought. She wasn't going to say anything however. She wanted to see what this was all about.

"Now, Johni, is that anyway to treat your wife?"

"Ex-wife."

"We should still be married," Brenda snapped.

"We're not," Johni responded. Brenda turned her attention towards Raven.

"I take it she hasn't told you about me yet," she queried Raven. As much as Raven wanted to say yes she couldn't.

"No she hasn't had time," Raven defended. Brenda laughed again.

"Hasn't had time. You have a wife but you don't have time to bring her up to anyone. Good Johni," Brenda barbed. Johni looked sick.

"Can we help you with something?" Raven asked. She wasn't sure what was going on but whatever it was she needed to be able to talk to Johni about it. Alone.

"Can you help me with anything?" Brenda asked sarcastically. "No dear, I don't think so." She added looking down her nose at Raven. Right then Raven's non-violent streak started to diminish. This woman was incredulous.

"Brenda, why don't you just leave before security comes to escort you out?" Johni asked. Now she's talking my language, Raven thought. She could tell Johni's patience was wearing thin. Brenda walked over to the bed and put her hand on Johni's. Johni instantly pulled away as if Brenda's touch had burned her. Brenda smiled.

"Now Johni, I know that you've been mad at me for a while but don't you think it's time to stop playing games?" Brenda's attitude was as if Johni had just been pouting. Raven looked at Johni and then at Brenda. She was becoming confused. Surely if Johni was really adamant about Brenda's presence this woman would not be so pushy. Maybe there was something here that she was missing. She took a step back in order to size up the situation.

"Brenda, why do you do this? Does the word no mean anything to you?" Johni asked. Brenda just smiled.

"What does mean something to me love is that you're mine and nothing or no one, (she looked at Raven for a second) is going to get in my way when it comes to you. Now I've made arrangements to bring you home when you're released...."

"What?" Johni asked.

"Excuse me?" Raven added.

"You heard me. Home, our home," Brenda answered. Johni sighed out loud. Raven couldn't believe how bold this woman was being. She couldn't take it anymore.

"You need to leave," Raven said sternly. Brenda looked at her and then dismissed her.

"I'll have the room downstairs made up..."

"I don't think you understood me," Raven said stepping up. "You need to leave. Johni has expressed an interest in your leaving and although I'm really enjoying watching you make a complete ass of yourself, I'd like to second that." Brenda was a little taken aback as was Johni. (Although she was enjoying this.) Raven stuck to her guns.

"Look you little bitch," Brenda started. "I have been married to this woman for six years now and what goes on between us goes on between us, got it!" Raven looked at Johni.

"Do you wish to correct that statement?" She asked.

"It was two years and she's been a pain in my ass ever since," Johni offered. Brenda's mouth dropped open. It was obvious that Johni had never gone quite this far before in defending herself to this woman.

"I've got that, now you get this. If you don't remove yourself I'll do it for you. And furthermore, that is Miss Bitch to you. Now leave!" Raven was pissed. She couldn't believe the nerve of this woman. Brenda started to open her mouth when she thought twice. Turning to leave she stopped at the door.

"When you're ready to come home, Johni, I'll be there. In the meantime you need to put your pet on a leash." With that Brenda left with Raven seething after her. A few moments later she turned to Johni.

"What the hell was that?" Raven asked. Johni shifted in the bed. She couldn't believe Brenda had left that easy.

"Brenda and I got married about six years ago. Our living together lasted all of a year," Johni offered. "You see how she is. I couldn't live with that."

"You divorced her?"

"I once loved her a great deal. She and I were high school sweethearts. I guess for a while I kept hoping that she would change. However, after a while, it became evident that she wouldn't. I divorced her a year after we split. I decided to never get married again," Johni answered. Raven was pleasantly surprised. If Johni wasn't anything else she was definitely honest. It took Raven a couple of minutes to digest Johni's answer.

"So.... do you still love her?" Raven asked carefully.

"I do but not in a way that I can share a life with her." Boy, Raven thought, she has this honesty thing down pat. Suddenly she wasn't so sure that her honesty was a good thing after all.

"If you planned to never get married again then why did you propose to me?" Raven asked, fishing. Johni smiled.

"I fell in love with you," Johni answered simply. Raven smiled.

"Come here," Johni said motioning for Raven to come back and join her on the bed. Raven lingered for a moment and when she felt she had made Johni wait long enough she went to her. They held onto each other for a minute and then Raven pulled back.

"Is she going to be a problem?" Raven asked. Johni laughed.

"She's nothing but wind. All Brenda ever does is follow me around telling me how much I need her."

"Not anymore she doesn't," Raven said looking at the door. Johni pulled her close.

"Listen brave warrior woman, you do not have to get territorial, I'm all yours. Johni said softly. Raven had to giggle.

"Well..." Raven started but Johni cut her off with a kiss.

* * *

It took the rest of the day to get Johni's things over to Raven's house. They had decided on Raven's place because it was bigger. Raven had supervised the moving of Johni's things herself but she had Mac, and his friend Joe, do the actual moving. When Raven first walked into Johni's house the first thing she noticed was how masculine everything was. All of the colors were earth tones. It was nice but it definitely needed a woman's touch. Raven hadn't planned to move all of Johni's things at first. She didn't want to seem too eager for her to move in but she quickly changed her mind. Hell Johni wasn't going any place. She was coming home now. Mac and Olie helped organize Johni's things at Raven's.

"I told you she was right for you," Olie was saying as she and Raven put Johni's clothes away. They boxed the things Andi had left behind. Raven smiled and made a mental note to somehow get them out of her place.

"She certainly is that," Raven agreed. Mac and Olie had both been singing the praises of their new relationship all day long.

"Is the therapy helping?" Mac asked bringing in the rest of Johni's computer.

"The doctors think so. She looks better, but we won't know until the sessions are over and they do another X-ray," Raven answered. She really believed in her heart that everything would be fine.

"That's great," Mac said going back to the truck. He was right it was great. Everything seemed to be falling into place.

* * *

Johni heard strands of Celine Dion in the distance. Where was she? A bump in the road jolted her and made her aware that she was in her Jeep. The Jeep? But that was totaled. The curve in the road up ahead seemed to move and Johni tried to adjust the Jeep's wheels to the road. Suddenly from around the curve a truck appeared. It seemed to head straight for her. She tried to avoid hitting it but when she adjusted the Jeep the truck adjusted as well. What was going on? Was this guy trying to kill her? Johni's headlights hit the truck a split second before the collision. Johni saw who was driving the truck. She couldn't believe it...

With a start Johni woke. She was sweating and her heart was going a mile a minute. She tried to remember the entire dream she'd been having. She recalled everything prior to seeing the face of the other driver and then she lost it. Who had been driving? Could it be possible that she had really seen the person who had hit her that night? Maybe her sub-conscious was trying to tell her something. Finally exhausted from trying to think, Johni fell back to sleep.

Raven did her best to organize Johni's things in a way that would make them easiest for her to get to. She spent the better part of the day and most of the evening getting things in place. It made her feel good to be needed. She had stocked the kitchen with things that she knew Johni would like and had even set aside part of the bathroom for Johni's personal things. Around eleven o'clock she showered and settled in with a book. The phone rang before she could get through the first page.

"Hello?" Raven said cautiously. She was always aware that the person on the other end of the phone could be Andi.

"Hi," came the voice on the other end. Raven had to smile. It was Johni.

"I thought you were supposed to be sleeping," Raven said.

"I was but I woke up and had to call you."

"Had to call me. Why would you have to call me?" Raven was fishing again.

"I woke up missing you so I had to call you. Is that okay? I didn't wake you did I?" Raven laughed.

"Good answer. No you didn't wake me. I just crawled into bed."

"Alone I hope."

"Of course."

"Do you miss me?" Johni asked quietly.

"You know I do," Raven answered.

"You know what I'd like to be doing right now?" Johni asked teasingly.

"Probably the same thing that I'd like to be doing," Raven baited. "But tell me anyway."

"Well.... for starters I'd love to have showered with you."

"Oh yeah? What else?"

"It would have been wonderful to have spent hours kissing and caressing your body."

"Hummmm..." Raven moaned. She was completely turned on and they hadn't been talking two minutes.

"I'm sure at that point you'd be wet, likely dripping."

"Yes..."

"I'm sure you taste wonderful."

"Oh? How can you be so sure?" Raven teased.

"Because when I hold you in my arms you always smell so good."

"So...what would you do with it once you found it baby?" Raven prodded.

"I'd taste it to confirm my suspicions."

"Only a taste?" Raven asked feeling herself start to peak.

"No," Johni answered, "I want the entire seven course meal, down to the last drop." Raven felt the rise in her womanhood and then the climax. After several moments she was completely relaxed.

"Satisfied?" Johni asked.

"You'll never know." Raven answered.

"I love you Raven. Good night."

"Good night, Johni. Sweet dreams"

Chapter 16

Raven got Johni comfortably settled on the couch.

"Are you sure you don't want to be in bed?" Raven asked for the fourth time. She wanted Johni to be comfortable.

"Yes, I'm sure. Raven I'm weak but I'm not crippled."

"Okay, okay. Do you want anything to eat?" Johni laughed.

"What I want is for you to come over here and sit next to me." Raven grinned and joined Johni on the couch. Johni put her arm around Raven and held her. Raven was in heaven.

"God this feels so good," Raven cooed.

"Yes it does," Johni agreed. They sat there for a long time just being together. After a while Johni broke the silence.

"Were you able to get all of my things?" She asked.

"All of the things you asked for and more," Raven answered. "I hope you don't mind, your house is kind of...well.... empty." Johni smiled.

"No. I just wanted to know if all of my computer stuff was here," Johni answered. Raven laughed.

"Having writing withdrawals?"

"Yep," Johni answered. She had to laugh too. "You don't mind, do you?"

"No, of course not. I love the fact that you write," Raven answered. "Whenever you get the urge, just do it."

"Okay," Johni said starting to get up." Raven gently pulled her back down.

"Not now though." Johni laughed.

"I know, I was just kidding," She was about to kiss Raven when the doorbell rang.

"Who could that be?" Raven said absently getting up to answer the door. She looked through the peephole. "Oh Lord!"

"Who is it?" Johni asked getting up to come see who it was. Raven was opening the door.

"What the hell do you want?" Raven asked. There in the doorway was Brenda.

"Now is that anyway to greet a guest?" Brenda asked stepping to go past Raven. Raven shifted into her way.

"You are not a guest," Raven answered. Johni stepped up behind Raven.

"Brenda what do you want?" Johni asked.

"We need to talk Johni," Brenda said ignoring Raven. This only fueled the fire Raven was already feeling.

"About what?" Johni asked. She too, was sounding impatient. Brenda looked at Raven.

"In private."

"I don't think so," Raven said stepping forward. "You are on our doorstep. Either you leave or I'll call the police and have you removed." Raven was holding her own and she was not going to move, that was obvious.

"I don't believe I addressed you," Brenda said to Raven before turning to Johni. Raven took a step back and slammed the door shut in Brenda's face. Johni had a surprised look on her face when she turned around.

"What?" Raven asked. "She wouldn't leave so I did the next best thing." Johni couldn't do anything but laugh. She put her arms around Raven and held her tight. The doorbell rang again. Raven swung the door open.

"WHAT?!" She bellowed. Brenda looked stunned.

"That was the rudest thing I have ever seen!" Brenda stammered. "Johni what has gotten into you to be with such a...a...thing?!" Raven slammed the door again. Johni laughed again and put her arms around Raven.

"I love you," she whispered in Raven's ear.

"I love you too." Raven returned.

Raven and Johni spent the rest of the day laying around and playing chess. They loved the game but hadn't had a decent challenge in months. They traded off wins and had a generally good time just being together. Raven couldn't remember when something had felt so right. After dinner they went into the living room and built a fire. Johni seemed very adept at building fires even with only one good hand. Raven enjoyed watching her. She noted how strong and confident Johni appeared. After starting the fire just so Johni fingered through the CD's and put on some music. If she's setting the mood, Raven thought, its working. Johni walked over and put her hand out for Raven's. Raven put her hand in Johni's and let herself be pulled up. Damn she's strong, Raven thought again.

"Dance with me," Johni said pulling Raven closer.

"Are you asking?" Raven asked.

"I'm telling you," Johni answered.

"Oh, okay," Raven said letting herself be pulled closer. Johni wrapped her up in her arms. That was the only way to describe what Johni was doing at this moment. It wasn't like being held, it was like being taken up. They danced and Raven marveled at how good a dancer Johni was, strong and rhythmic. Johni noticed the smile on Raven's face.

"I know, who would have guessed, I have rhythm." Raven laughed.

"That is not what I was thinking," Raven protested.

"Yeah sure," Johni said laughing. The thought had run through Raven's mind.

"You're a good dancer," Raven countered. Johni smiled.

"I do all right."

"You do better than all right," Raven said.

"You're just biased," Johni countered.

"Yeah, maybe," Raven teased. Johni laughed. They

danced through the whole CD. Johni had chosen Barry White, which pleased Raven very much. They didn't have to speak. They just held each other and swayed to the music. After the CD ended Johni replaced it with another and they sat down on the couch to hold hands and enjoy the fire.

"I love you," Raven whispered. Johni kissed her. The passion in her kiss was evident. She was hungry for Raven. She hadn't felt this desired in a long time. Raven released herself to Johni. Letting her body feel all of the sensations that Johni's kisses provoked. Then slowly Johni's hand began to explore Raven's body. She had the gentlest touch. It was as if her hand was feeling into Raven's very soul. She reveled in the electricity that was coursing from Johni's hand into her body. She hardly noticed that Johni hadn't used the other one. As she touched Johni's body, she felt the strength through her clothes. Suddenly with a passion that she had thought long dead Raven needed to be as close as she could get to Johni. She tore at the buttons on Johni's shirt. It didn't stop Johni or for that matter even slow her down. Johni began to remove Raven's clothes. They both stepped out of what remained of their clothes as the fire light danced on their bodies. The music gave fury to the fire they were both feeling inside. Johni let go of Raven and stepped back.

"What's wrong?" Raven asked suddenly worried. Johni

smiled.

"Nothing. I just want to see you. I want to see what you look like."

"Do you like what you see?" Raven asked teasingly, already knowing the answer.

"Oh yes," Johni whispered, "very much so." Johni took a step forward and cautiously scooped Raven up into her arms. Raven marveled at her strength. She didn't seem to be hindered by the injured hand at all. Johni carried her to the bedroom and lay Raven gently down on the bed.

"Make love to me Johni," Raven whispered.

"Done," Johni whispered back with a smile. Raven lay back anticipating what was to come. She moaned as Johni's hands explored her body for the first time. She quivered as Johni kissed her neck and shoulders.

"Oh Johni," Raven breathed. Johni's fever for her increased and her passion intensified. She worked her mouth down to Raven's nipples and gently sucked and pulled on first one and then the other. Raven could barely contain herself. She cried out.

"Oh what are you doing to me?" Johni lifted her head and whispered.

"Only what you deserve my lady." With that Johni traced Raven's stomach with her tongue. She worked it from her shoulders to her nipples to her navel. Raven would swear that Johni kissed every square inch of her.

Her insides were on fire. As if that weren't enough, Johni talked to her the whole time. Savoring the moment for as long as she could, Raven finally cried out.

"Johni, please."

"Are you ready? Are you ready for me?" Johni teased.

"Oh yes, baby, I'm ready." Johni moved her mouth from Raven's stomach to her thighs. Raven thought she would lose her mind.

"Oh Lord," she whispered.

"You're so soft and you smell so good, baby," Johni cooed. Raven felt an electric shock with every kiss. She felt Johni's hot breath on her. A moment later Johni's tongue had found its way. Raven's cried out in ecstasy. Johni moaned as she ran her tongue through Raven's wet mound, licking and sucking gently. Raven couldn't think; she couldn't be anywhere but here. Johni's tongue prodded Raven's pearl into erection.

"You taste so good," Johni said as her tongue found its way into Raven. Raven's body quivered. She felt as though she would explode any minute. Her pearl moved into Johni's mouth with the same rhythm with which Johni's tongue moved.

"You're so wet," Johni said devouring Raven. She cried out. She couldn't contain herself. She had lost complete control.

"Oh, baby," Raven moaned. Johni was only spurned

further. Raven felt herself approaching organism.

"Johni, I want you inside me." She pleaded. Johni rose up and climbed the length of Raven's body. Kissing various spots as she went. When she reached Raven's face Johni kissed her with a hunger and passion that Raven was positive she'd never felt before. The taste of her made Raven moan with pleasure. Johni then entered Raven first with one finger and then two. Raven thrust upward to meet Johni's rhythm.

"Oooh baby," Raven cried out and Johni probed deeper. Raven's hips moved faster. She knew that she had lost control but she didn't care.

"Please Johni, I need to touch you too." Johni excitedly readjusted herself so that Raven could reach her. She too cried out as Raven entered her. Raven couldn't believe how wet Johni was. And her pearl, it was like nothing she had never felt before. It was hard as a rock.

"Oh, Johni," Raven cried. They touched each other, playing and caressing until they were on the verge of complete satisfaction. With hunger and passion they climaxed together, both crying out in ecstasy. Raven felt her insides spasm again and again. She climaxed once, then twice and finally a third time. Johni too exploded. Both, finally spent, collapsed in each other's arms.

"I love you, Raven," Johni said out of breath.

"I love you too, baby," Raven whispered. They lay in

each other's arms, deeply in love and satisfied. Soon they were fast asleep.

* * *

Outside the window Andi fumed. She's never made love to me like that, she thought. How dare she give herself to that bitch! Sweat poured from Andi's brow. She leaned on the fence. Reaching into her pocket she pulled out her trusty knife. She had taken this knife off her father's body before it had gotten cold. Opening the knife, she ran it across her left arm harder and harder until small beads of blood appeared. She watched the window to the room she'd once shared with Raven and continued mutilating herself for almost an hour. By the time she was finished she had a long gash in her left forearm. It bled freely but Andi didn't seem to notice. She just continued to watch the window. Closing the knife, she put it back in her pocket. She waited patiently for several more hours, just watching the window and waiting. By the time her watch read 2a.m. the moon was high in the sky and cast a dim glow over the night. All was quiet except for the occasional dog barking. Andi made her way around to the front of the house. She stopped briefly to rub the back of her left leg. It ached from standing so long. Stretching it out Andi surveyed the neighborhood. Everything was dark. She crept to the front door along the house to make use of the shadows for cover. She was banking on the fact that Raven was so forgetful when she had a lot on her mind. Andi was sure that with all the time Raven had spent with that dyke, Andrews, she would have forgotten to re-key the locks. Andi still had her keys. Carefully inserting the key into the lock, Andi crossed her fingers and gently turned the key. It clicked. She was in. She eased the door open.

The house was dark. Hopefully Raven hadn't moved too much. The last thing she wanted to do was trip over something in the dark. Stepping over the threshold she stopped. Damn! She whispered. She'd forgotten her bag in the truck. Padding back out across the lawn Andi reached into the back of her truck and removed a leather overnight bag. It was the one Raven had given her for Christmas last year. The damn thing had finally come in handy. Creeping back across the lawn Andi again crossed the threshold of her former home. In the moonlight she could make out the living room furniture. At least she wouldn't fall over anything. Moving quietly Andi padded down the hallway to the bedroom. The door was slightly cracked. Peering in she could make out the sleeping figures of Raven and the dyke in bed together. For a moment she felt the urge to burst in and rip the two of them apart with her knife but she controlled it. She couldn't lose it now. That was not part of the "Plan". She turned and headed for the kitchen. She had work to do.

Chapter 17

Raven woke up wrapped in what seemed to be the warmest, safest arms she'd ever had the pleasure of being held in. The memory of the night before brought a smile to her face as she snuggled in closer to Johni. Johni stirred just slightly before settling back into a deep sleep. Everything was going to be all right now. Raven could feel it. Nothing or no one could come between them. Last night would be etched in her memory forever. Raven had been more than satisfied with Johni's abilities to please her. The whole experience was more than she had dared hope for. They had achieved a oneness that few people experienced in a lifetime. Raven had to giggle at her eternal romanticism. Her giggles woke Johni.

"What is so funny?" Johni asked gathering Raven further into her arms.

"Nothing."

"You're laughing at nothing? Is there a family illness I should know about?"

"Very funny," Raven said taking a swipe at Johni over her shoulder.

"Spousal abuse too. What have I gotten myself into?" Johni teased.

"Are you going to leave me now?"

"I don't know, think I should?" Johni asked

thoughtfully.

"You couldn't if you wanted to."

"Oh yeah? Why is that?"

"It's too good."

"It what?" Johni prodded.

"It, me," Raven answered with a giggle. Johni readjusted herself so that she lay on top of Raven, mindful not to let all of her weight down. After all Raven wasn't a very big woman.

"It? I don't remember an 'it'," Johni said sliding down the length of Raven's body coming to rest between her legs. Raven squirmed a little.

"Johni, I haven't had a shower," Raven half protested.

"And...."

"And, you should wait until I have showered," Raven insisted.

"I want to see this "it"." Johni started kissing Raven's inner thighs. Raven tried once more to protest but Johni wasn't having it. She continued to kiss everywhere but where Raven desired her to. Raven's body voluntarily moved upward to meet Johni's kisses. She moaned softly which only served to fuel Johni's desire for her.

"Baby, please," Raven groaned softly. Johni teased her further flicking Raven's pearl slightly with the tip of her tongue. Raven felt a burning sensation within her body. She wanted Johni so badly. She had never felt this way before. Finally Johni's passion overwhelmed her and she hungrily took Raven into her mouth. Raven cried out as Johni took everything she had. She moved in rhythm to Johni for as long as she could.

"Can you feel me? Can you feel me," Raven breathed. Johni devoured Raven until she finally cried out in pleasure. Wave after wave of orgasm over took Raven and for a time she lost all trace of time or space. Johni finally lay back, out of breath and smiling. Raven took this opportunity to crawl onto Johni and kiss her passionately. Johni responded instantly. Raven knew that Johni needed release as well. They moved their bodies together in perfect time as they shared the most wonderful kisses. Raven moved her hand downward in order to pleasure Johni. She touched Johni's pearl and then took it into her fingers. She gently kneaded it until it swelled larger than any other Raven had ever felt. Finally Johni let go and orgasm came with the force of a storm. She couldn't help but smile.

"What are you grinning at?" Johni asked, out of breath.

"You."

"What about me?" Johni asked turning towards Raven.

"You come hard." They both laughed.

"I don't know about you lady," Johni said hugging Raven.

"You love me," Raven said softly.

"That I do," Johni responded kissing Raven on top of the head.

"How about breakfast?" Raven asked, getting up. "I'm starving."

"Okay. Do I get to order?"

"No. The doctor gave me a list of foods you can eat and I'll be willing to bet you weren't going to ask for any of them," Raven answered. She was determined to keep Johni healthy.

"Oh damn, I knew this would happen," Johni whined.

"What?" Raven asked.

"You and the Doc are in this together."

"Yes we are. We want to keep you around. Now get up and I'll get breakfast and your meds," Raven said heading for the kitchen. Johni lay back and smiled.

"Get up!" Raven said sticking her head back in the door, "now."

"All right already."

Raven had the kitchen stocked with all of the things the doctor said Johni would need. Her sessions had been cut down but the doctor reminded them that a constant watch on Johni's health would be necessary. Raven intended to do just that. She made a breakfast of fresh fruit and bagels. She heard the shower start in the back of the house and for a moment considered joining Johni in the shower. She quickly decided against it reasoning that it would only get things started again. They really needed to get some work done. Since Johni had therapy tomorrow, Raven felt that they should work on getting settled in today. She busied herself with cleaning the kitchen until Johni came in.

"I'm clean now," Johni said hugging Raven.

"You smell like it too."

"Thanks," Johni said sitting down at the table. "What's for grub?" Raven put the plates of fruit and bagels on the table.

"Oh," Johni said feigning disappointment.

"Eat," Raven demanded, "and take these." She handed Johni her medicine, two pills and a small cup of liquid.

"I don't know why I have to drink the stuff in the cup," Johni complained. "I feel like a little kid."

"Just take it," Raven ordered. Johni downed the medicine with a grimace.

"Yuk! It tastes awful. I don't remember it tasting bad in the hospital." Raven laughed.

They sat and drank coffee, eating the food that Raven had prepared, laughing and talking. After a while the conversation took a more serious turn.

"Have you thought anymore about the accident?" Raven inquired chewing on a piece of bagel.

"What about it?"

"Have you thought about who it may have been that hit you?"

"Once and in a while I wonder," Johni answered. "I don't know what I'd do if I knew."

"It bothers me, you know, that someone could just leave you like that not knowing whether you were dead or alive," Raven said and a chill ran down her spine. Johni reached over and grabbed her hand.

"It bothers me too, Raven, but we will probably never know who it was."

"It had to be a very cruel person. I guess I'd just really like to know what kind of person would do a thing like that and why." Johni squeezed Raven's hand.

"I know. At least I'm still alive and here with you now." She reassured. Raven looked up and smiled.

"I love you, Johni."

"I love you too Raven." They sat smiling at each other and enjoying the moment together.

"Well," Johni finally said, "are we going to do anything today or do you want to go back to bed?"

"Pervert."

"Yeah, and...."

"You are relentless," Raven said laughing.

"That's what they say," Johni said getting up from the table. She hugged Raven. When she let go Raven noticed a strange look on her face.

"What?" Raven asked sarcastically. Johni squirmed.

"Can I go and hook up my computer?" Raven had to

laugh.

"Yes of course you can," She said.

"Great!" Johni bounded off towards the bedroom.

"Johni," Raven called out. Johni stopped in the bedroom doorway.

"Yeah?"

"Don't forget about me," Raven said smiling.

"Not a chance, little lady." Raven blushed and set about cleaning the house. She started in the kitchen and worked her way into the living room. She was picking up the CD's from the night before when something shiny at the end of the couch caught her attention. She leaned over to look closer and couldn't believe what she saw. There in a small pile, broken into several pieces, were the disks from last night. Hurriedly, Raven opened the CD covers she was holding in her hand. Sure enough they were empty. She picked up the pieces. They were two of her favorites too. She walked to the bedroom with them.

"Johni, look." She held the CD's out for Johni to examine.

"What happened?" Johni asked taking the disks.

"I don't know. I found them on the floor next to the couch," Raven answered. "Could we have broken them last night?" Johni looked perplexed.

"I don't think so." Raven was about to say something else when the doorbell rang.

"I'll get it," Raven said and headed for the front door.

"Okay." Johni answered absently. She was still trying to figure out what happened to the CD's. Raven went to the door and opened it. A man was standing on the porch.

"May I help you?" Raven asked.

"Yes ma'am. Is Andi here?"

"No, she doesn't live here anymore," Raven, answered. Where had she seen this man before?

"I'm Dave, the guy who dropped off Andi's bill with you a while back. Did she get it?" That's where she had seen him. She looked back into the foyer. The bill was still on the table.

"No, she didn't. But I'll tell you what, I'll try and get it to her," Raven offered. "She moved out shortly after you came by last."

"Thanks, I appreciate it. I have a family to feed and I really need the money," he said, shifting on his feet. He looked like a nice young man. "Normally I wouldn't have done this type of job but I felt bad for her because she was so afraid her father would find out."

"Her father?" Raven asked surprised.

"Yeah, she said that if he found out that she had wrecked her truck he'd kill her. Usually, we are required by law to report cars we fix that have been in an accident but she seemed honest enough. Anyway, thanks." Dave left and Raven closed the door, baffled. Johni came to see what was prompting such a long conversation between Raven and the man at the door.

"Is everything all right?" Johni asked.

"I don't know. That was a mechanic who worked on Andi's truck. He said she told him that her father would be mad if he knew she had wrecked the truck."

"So."

"Andi's father has been dead for six years."

"Maybe she was just trying to get the guy to give her a break," Johni offered.

"Maybe. Funny thing is I don't remember Andi wrecking her truck in any way." Raven walked over to the foyer table and picked up the envelope the young man had left the first time. Opening it she found an itemized list of what had been wrong with Andi's truck along with the copy of a note from her stating the same thing Dave had just told her. From the looks of it Andi's truck had been in bad shape.

"That's strange," Raven, said out loud, "she never mentioned this."

"Maybe she was embarrassed," Johni offered.

"Maybe...." Raven said looking over the bill again. "That bitch...."

"What? What's wrong?" Johni asked concerned. Raven was pissed.

"The date, Johni, look at the date." Johni took the bill

from Raven. She didn't understand.

"All the trouble we were having and she took the time to fix that damn truck," Raven answered. "Shows you how really important I was doesn't it?" Jamie saw what she was referring to. The date on the invoice was the day after she'd had her accident. She had to agree with Raven. It was a little insensitive.

"Well, aren't you glad you're with me now?" Johni chimed. She was trying to make Raven feel better. Raven looked up for a moment and then Johni watched the clouds of anger clear from her eyes as a smile spread across her face.

"Yeah, I guess I am lucky, huh?" She put her arms around Johni's neck and hugged her. "Thanks," she whispered.

"For what?"

"Loving me," Raven cooed.

"That's my job," Johni said kissing the end of her nose. Raven smiled and let go.

"Better get back to work I guess," she said turning to leave. She'd reached the living room door when she turned back to Johni. "What about those?" She indicated the CD's.

"I don't know," Johni said examining them again. "We must have broken them though, unless you have a bogeyman," she offered with an evil smile.

"Don't say that. I'll have nightmares," Raven whined. Johni laughed and handed the broken CD's to Raven.

"Here, I'll buy you new ones." Raven took the CD's, dumped the in the trash and went back to her work. Every now and then she would check on Johni. She was diligently working away at her computer with her good hand. Raven smiled in spite of her slight jealousy. It was good to see her work. After Raven cleaned the living room and the front bathroom she decided that it was time to get back to her own computer. It had been a month since she had done any work and it was time to get back to it. She was on her way to the front bedroom that she'd converted into an office when she heard a crashing sound from the back bedroom. She raced down the hallway to discover Johni on her knees at the bathroom door. She rushed to her side.

"What happened?" She cried reaching for Johni. Johni looked dazed. She helped her up and to the bed. "What's wrong honey?" Johni shook her head.

"I don't know. I was going to the bathroom when I got dizzy and fell." Raven had been afraid of this.

"You started moving around too soon," she scolded. "I should have made you stay in bed." Johni favored her with one of her infamous, give-me-a-break looks.

"I'm fine, just a little tired."

"Get undressed and into bed," Raven demanded. Johni

looked at her for a second and started to laugh. Raven stood glaring at her. "What are you laughing at?"

"You, acting like Mama Cass. You need to quit." Raven tried to look angry but started laughing too. She hugged Johni again.

"I just want you to be okay," She said stroking Johni's hair.

"I know. Okay, I'll lie down but I'm going to read." Johni got into bed she was sweating slightly. "It's strange. I'm feeling really weak. Maybe I did get up too soon." Raven tucked her in and went to the bathroom to get a cool towel. By the time she got back Johni was fast asleep. She sat on the bed with her for a while, concerned. That's it; she would have to make Johni take it easier. Satisfied that Johni would sleep for a while, Raven went to work on her accounts in the office.

* * *

Andi rented a white four-door sedan and drove to the house. She parked across the street, several houses down. It was already 3pm but that couldn't have been avoided. After all, she needed to get some sleep. Raven's MG was in the driveway so she knew they were there. After what she did to the dykes Jeep, it wasn't likely to be sitting up in the driveway anytime soon. Andi smiled. It was really too bad that she didn't go with it.

"If you'd done it right she would have died." It was her father's voice.

"Shut up. You couldn't have done better," Andi responded. She glanced around to make sure that no one spotted her talking.

"Now you know that's not true. I was the master. You learned everything you know from me. You're just too stupid to follow directions."

"Killed you didn't I." It was a statement.

"YOU GOT LUCKY!" The voice roared. Andi laughed.

"Doesn't do you any good to yell at me now."

"No? I can still talk to her. That's what I'll do, Andi. I'll talk to her and tell her how bad you've been and she'll beat you again." The voice mocked. Andi glanced around nervously. She didn't see her. He was lying. "You know how she gets." Indeed she did. She knew exactly how she got. After all, she was still around even after he was gone, screaming at her and hitting her whenever she'd got the inkling. She was always telling Andi that she was no good. Andi covered her ears.

"Leave me alone!" She said loudly. A man walking his dog glanced briefly in her direction but quickly turned his head when she glared at him. The voice continued to mock her.

"Why don't you just kill them? Why are you wasting

time with these games? Just go in there tonight and carve 'em up like a couple of prize turkeys."

"I don't want to! I want to see them suffer! NOW LEAVE ME ALONE!" She couldn't take hearing his voice anymore. She looked at the cigarette lighter. She knew what she had to do. Turning the ignition on she popped the lighter in. After several minutes it popped back out and she pulled it loose. Holding it up she made sure that the circle in the center was indeed glowing orange. It was. Holding it horizontal she inserted her left forefinger into the open end. After several seconds she heard a sizzling sound followed by the smell of burnt flesh. She held her finger still until she felt the lighter cool slightly. With the cooling of the lighter came the diminishing of the voice. Pain always made him go away. Returning the lighter to its rightful place she blew on the injured finger. Now she could think straight. She hated him but she was afraid of her. Who could blame her? The old lady was a nut, loony as a bird. She barked for goodness sake. Barked. Andi turned her attention back to the house. Everything was quiet. She wondered if they were having problems yet. She smiled. It was just amazing the house hold uses for rat poisoning. A car turned the corner and Andi hunkered down. The last thing she needed was for someone to get suspicious. 5:15pm, damn these longer days, she thought to herself. Another car turned the corner. The street was getting too busy. Andi started the car and made a U-turn in the street. She'd go get something to eat but later, when it was dark, she'd be back.

Chapter 18

Johni slept most of the afternoon. She didn't wake up until six and she was still groggy. Raven was concerned. She made soup for dinner and set Johni's medicine out.

"Soup?" Johni asked carefully. She didn't want to offend Raven. "Hospital food, huh?" Raven looked up at Johni.

"You need to go easier, don't you think?" She asked, her face a mask of concern.

"I'm going to be okay, Raven. I'm just tired, that's all," Johni insisted. Raven looked skeptical but relaxed a little.

"At least eat the soup."

"If I must. Look at this, haven't been together two days and she's already starving me." Raven laughed. Johni ate and took her medicine. Then they moved to the couch. Johni was already looking worn out again.

"You're tired, huh?" Raven asked brushing Johni's hair from her face.

"Well, a little. I'm sorry. I don't know what's wrong with me." Raven laughed.

"Well maybe getting hit by a truck had something to do with it," she offered.

"Maybe. Would you mind if I went to bed early?" Johni asked. "I am really beat and maybe if I go to sleep early I'll feel better in the morning." Raven nodded.

I'll go with you." Johni was touched.

"You don't have to."

"I want to," Raven answered. They both got up. "I'll check the doors."

"That's my job," Johni whined. Raven rubbed her head.

"You can take over he-woman when you're feeling better. Now go I'll be there in a minute." Johni reluctantly went to bed and Raven went about the business of checking doors and windows. Everything looked okay. She started for the bedroom when she remembered that the ferns needed to go out onto the front porch. She meant to do that earlier. She retrieved the ferns from the living room and took them to the front door. Unlocking it, she stepped outside into the night air. It was a brisk evening and the moon shone just past full. She took a deep breath and turned to get the ferns. She sat them just outside the door. The cool night air would do them some good. Taking one last breath she turned went back inside and locked the door.

* * *

As she heard the faint click of the door lock Andi let out the breath she'd been holding. That was close. She had no idea that they were still up. She had been watching the house for hours and had seen no movement inside. She was just about to go in again when she heard the door start to open. She had managed to hurriedly throw herself beside the porch and stand very still. Raven had come to put the ferns out. She had been within arm's reach. Part of her ached to hold Raven again, the part that was tucked in a faraway place in her heart. Her other self, the one her mother called, the "demon child", was in control now. This part of her wanted to kill Raven, to cut her extremities off one at a time and watch her slowly bleed to death. Quietly, Andi padded back across the lawn. She had taken great pains to dress so that no one would detect her in the shadows. Ironically, she was wearing clothes that Raven had bought for her. Her black sweats and the Black Pumas she had gotten for her birthday in January. It was actually her favorite outfit. She settled in the bushes to the right of the house. She would have to be patient yet again.

* * *

"By the time Raven got to the bedroom Johni was asleep. She crawled in next to her and curled up around her body. Johni snuggled into her. Raven glanced over Johni at the alarm clock and noted that it was already ten. It was later than she had thought. Somewhere in the distance she thought she heard a noise. She listened to see if she would hear it again but she didn't. It didn't take long for Raven to fall fast asleep.

Andi could have kicked herself. She had prowled back

up to the door and knocked over the ferns, both of them. She dashed back into the shadows but no one emerged.

"Fuck, fuck, fuck!" She said under her breath. She had to be more careful. Waiting another full hour, Andi finally proceeded with her plan. She was behind schedule and a little irritated. Carefully unlocking the door she slipped in quietly. She listened but heard nothing. The first place she headed for was the bedroom. Cracking the door she looked in on the two sleeping figures in the bed.

"No nookie tonight, eh, Raven. Lover girl toooooo tired," she whispered. She watched Raven sleep. The rise and fall of her chest was driving Andi crazy. Part of her wanted to fuck her and part of her wanted to fucking kill her. In her twisted world she imagined herself sneaking in and standing next to the bed.

She saw the surprised look on Andrew's face as she plunged her knife into her heart. She then grabbed Raven before Raven could realize what was happening and shoved her face into the hole in Andrews's chest. She almost drown Raven in Andrew's warm blood pumping out of the chest wound she herself had just inflicted. Then just as Raven gasped Andi pulled her up and tasted the blood on Raven's lips. She could see the blood fresh and crimson. She marveled at the metallic taste. She watched the terror in Raven's face as she plunged the knife up into her vagina so that, if by some chance she got away, (you just never knew about these things) she would never fuck again.

Andi stood lost in thought until a sound startled her. Andrews had turned over and laid a protective arm over Raven. Andi smiled thinking, if I wanted to do anything, that wouldn't help. Reluctantly, Andi turned and headed down the hallway. First she stopped in Raven's office. She turned on the computer monitor and brought up Raven's word processor. She typed in her message and then turned off the monitor. When Raven turned on the monitor tomorrow the first thing she would she is her message. Leaving the office, she went into the kitchen. She opened the refrigerator, removed Johni's liquid medicine and added one more drop of the liquefied rat poison.

"She thought she was tired today," Andi whispered. She replaced the bottle and quietly closed the refrigerator door. Andi smiled to herself as she made her way to the front door. She stopped briefly to look back down the dark hallway. "You just never know what people might do, Raven," she whispered. "You just don't know."

* * *

Raven woke up at six o'clock refreshed and ready for the day. She cleaned up and made breakfast. She surprised Johni with breakfast in bed.

"Wake up sleepy head," she chimed setting the tray

down on the bedside table.

"What's this?" Johni asked sitting up. Raven smiled and unfolded a napkin putting it on Johni's lap.

"Breakfast for you."

"This is nice Raven," Johni was pleased and it was obvious, it made Raven feel good.

"You're welcome. Now come on, eat." She had made bacon and eggs. Johni ate like she hadn't eaten in months. It did Raven's heart good to see her eat like that. When she was done she just sat smiling.

"That was nice. Thank you." She put a hand out to Raven who took it without hesitation. Johni pulled her close and hugged her. Raven couldn't help but feel the strength in Johni's arms. She felt as though she fit perfectly into her body. They were made for each other. Johni pulled her back and kissed her. Raven couldn't help but get lost. Johni kissed her passionately. She briefly prayed that Johni would never stop kissing her like that. She knew in her heart that she wouldn't. Johni finally took a breath.

"Wow," Raven said, "all that for breakfast? What do I get for lunch?" She teased. Johni laughed.

"Who knows," she spouted back. "So what's up for today?"

"How do you feel?" Raven asked suddenly getting serious. Johni smiled at her concern.

"Fine. I feel real good."

"Have you taken your medicine?" Raven asked looking at the tray. The cup and pills were still there. "No," she said answering her own question. Johni looked reluctantly at the medicine.

"I really would like to forgo those for this morning. They make me tired and I'd like to stay up for a little while." Raven looked skeptical but had to admit she couldn't blame Johni.

"Okay. But you need to take them later, all right?"

"Oh all right," Johni said in mock protest. "So what's up today?"

"I need to get some work done," Raven answered. "I probably have a few clients who think I've dropped off the face of the planet.

"Great, then I can get some work done too," Johni said hopping out of bed. Raven noted how much more alive she looked today. She got up, kissed Johni on the cheek and went to her office. Sitting in her chair she heard the shower come on. She smiled mischievously. Oh if you only knew about that shower, Johni. She let out a giggle. Raven reached over and hit the on switch to her monitor. She turned around looking for her client book. When she turned back around she couldn't believe her eyes. There on the screen was a clipart image of the grim reaper with her face on it. The caption read," How does it feel to bring death to others?" She rubbed her eyes and looked again to make sure she was seeing right. Sure enough, it was still there. She heard the shower water go off. She sat there for a moment and just as she decided to go get Johni she appeared in the doorway. The look on Raven's face stopped her.

"What's wrong?" She asked. Raven pointed to the screen. Johni looked at the screen and then at Raven.

"Who would send you that?" She asked. Raven shook her head.

"I don't know, probably some sicko. Maybe it's a sick joke from Andi? I just don't know." Johni stood looking at the image. She didn't like it at all.

"Can you find out where it came from?" Johni asked. Something told her that they needed to deal with this.

"There should be an e-mail record," Raven offered. After searching here and there in her computer she sat back. She looked concerned.

"What?" Johni asked.

"It didn't come from anywhere."

"What do you mean? It had too. I don't pull shit like that." Johni protested.

"No, someone had to sit here and do this, probably Andi. I haven't turned the computer on since she left. She probably did it before she left," Raven answered. Johni was annoyed.

"Not very funny. She must have been a piece of work."

"Oh she was, believe me, she was." Johni shook her head.

"Well get rid of that and go on with your work. She can't touch you now. Not with me around," Johni stated. Raven got up and slid her arms around Johni's neck.

"My protector."

"And don't you forget it," Johni said kissing her. "Now get to work woman." Raven laughed and sat down. She looked at the image a moment longer then pushed the delete button. The picture disappeared.

Chapter 19

Raven worked on her computer for the rest of the afternoon. Johni worked for a couple of hours, slept for a couple of hours and was now working again. That was to be expected. It was noon before she convinced Johni to take her medicine. She understood Johni's feelings though, her mother used to have to wrestle her to take medicines too. As evening fell Raven stopped and prepared them a light dinner. Johni worked until Raven called her. She was putting the salad on the table when Johni came in. Johni was dragging again already. She looked irritated as she plopped down into a chair.

"How are you feeling?" Raven asked taking the chair opposite her. Johni looked up and smiled weakly.

"I look that bad, huh?"

"No," Raven defended, "you just look tired." She reached across the table and took Johni's hand.

"I guess I'm just tired of being tired." She answered squeezing Raven's hand. "That medicine's got me really dragging ass." Raven sympathized but was about to stress the importance of taking the medicine when Johni put up a hand in defense. "I know, I know, I still need to take it." Raven smiled and offered Johni salad.

"A peace offering?" She whispered.

"Accepted," Johni answered. They both laughed.

Raven marveled at how good it was to hear laughter in this house after so many arguments. All she and Andi had done was argue. Andi. Thinking about her brought something important to mind.

"I need to see if I can find Andi," she said carefully.

"For what?" Johni asked stuffing a fork full of salad into her mouth.

"I promised that man that I would try to get that bill to her," she answered. "Is that okay with you?" Johni considered for a moment and then nodded her head yes.

"I don't have a problem with it. It's not like she's a threat to us." Raven smiled. Such confidence, she liked that.

"I need to call everywhere I think she might be."

"You also need to be careful," Johni added.

"Andi would never hurt me."

"Yeah, maybe, but being careful can't hurt. You said she was acting a little nuts last time you saw her." Raven had to admit Johni had a point. She never thought Andi would have spoken to her the way she had. It had surprised her. It was strange how you could live with someone for so long and not really know who they were. Johni cleared her throat.

"So where do we start?" She asked a surprised Raven.

"You're going to help?" Raven asked.

"Of course I am."

"Great. I appreciate that," Raven breathed. She hadn't wanted to see Andi alone. Johni smiled.

"Raven, the way I figure it is this, we are a couple. I'm going to marry you very soon and we should tackle this type of thing together. Andi has been acting up and you don't know what she might do. She's probably hurting and people do stupid things when they hurt." Raven was pleased. She really admired Johni's attitude.

"Well, I'm not going to let Andi be a pain in our asses forever." Raven said getting up and pacing a little. She didn't know why thinking of Andi made her a little nervous. "As soon as I talk to her about this I'm severing all ties." Johni nodded in agreement.

"So where do we start?" Johni asked again.

"With the phone," Raven answered. "I'll go get my phone book." They spent the better part of the morning on the phone with everyone Raven knew. Raven had spoken with people she hadn't seen nor heard from for years. She was pulling out all the stops. She wanted to find Andi and finish her business. She figured she could drop the rest of her stuff off with her as well. No one she spoke to knew where Andi was.

"Maybe she left the area?" Johni offered.

"I don't think so. She has a sister who lives in Southern California but she's estranged from her. Her mother lives here."

"What about her mother?" Raven laughed and Johni favored her with a confused look. "What's so funny? You did just say she had one didn't you?"

"Oh, she has one all right. They don't get along. Her mother is, pardon my French, a bitch," Raven answered.

"So...I take it they don't get along." Johni laughed.

"No, not at all. Andi's mother is homophobic and that's just the beginning. She gives Andi the worse time in the world. She really hates me."

"You? Why would she hate you?" Johni asked. She couldn't imagine anyone hating Raven.

"I'm not sure. Last year we had a huge blowout on the phone. Andi was always telling me what her mother said about me, none of it very nice," Raven recalled. "She called me a few names, said that I only wanted Andi for my young trophy, things like that."

"So, she's not only homophobic but prejudiced as well."

"Yes, the whole family is. I received a nasty phone call from her sister too. They're a religious family. I think that might have something to do with it."

"That is really a shame," Johni said shaking her head.

"Yes, it really is. Andi's mother abused her so badly that I always felt terrible for her." Raven said flipping through the pages of her phone book. She had tried over the years to soften the stress Andi's family had put on her but Andi always seem to be fighting her on it. It was as if she enjoyed being hurt by her family. In the last year or so Raven finally gave up and tried to stay out of Andi's family business. That seemed to be the best way to avoid the grief Andi put her through if she said anything remotely negative about family.

"What are you thinking about?" Johni asked, breaking Raven's train of thought. Raven smiled. It was so nice to have someone who cared about what she was thinking.

"Oh, Andi and her family and all that," Raven answered. "It's really strange the way people can get."

"I think you should call her mother anyway," Johni offered.

"Why?"

"Maybe Andi went to her and made amends. She could have blamed the whole relationship on you or something." Raven hadn't considered that. If Andi were desperate she might do that.

"Maybe you're right; I'll look for the number." Raven found the number in the kitchen drawer. Just days before they separated Andi had put the number in there along with a list of others. She reasoned that if anything ever happened to her Raven would need the numbers. Andi was morbid like that sometimes.

"Here it is." Raven said waving the paper so that Johni could see it. She dialed Andi's mother. After two rings the phone was picked up.

"Hello?" The voice on the other end said. Raven could tell right away that it was Andi's mother. The woman always sounded so condescending.

"Hello, Mrs. Lancaster? This is Raven, Andi's roommate," Raven said carefully. She stopped and waited for the anticipated click on the other end of the line. It didn't come.

"Yes?" Raven was surprised; she almost didn't know what to say next.

"Mrs. Lancaster, have you seen Andi?"

"No." It was obvious that this woman was not going to have an actual conversation with her.

"Would you happen to know where she is?" Raven pressed. "I have some of her things and I need to get them to her." There was silence on the other end of the line for a time.

"Mrs. Lancaster?"

"I'm here, Andi's not. She called and said something about you two breaking up and asked me for money but I don't know where she is."

"Money? Mrs. Lancaster if you don't mind my asking, how much money?" Raven asked. She was surprised; Andi had always had a sizable bank account. Maybe Johni was right and Andi was leaving the area.

"Two thousand dollars," Raven was shocked.

"For what," she blurted out?

"She wouldn't say which is why she didn't get it. I'm not out to just give my money away. I told her if she came home I'd help her but she refused," Mrs. Lancaster spit out. It was obvious that she was not at all pleased with Andi.

"Mrs. Lancaster did Andi say anything about where she was or where she was going? I really need to find her," Raven asked.

"Well, she didn't say exactly. She asked me for Lori's address and said something about wiring the money to Western Union." Andi's sister Lori lived in the LA area in southern California. Raven doubted that Andi would go that far, but maybe...

"I think she's staying in the city," Andi's mother chimed in.

"Why would you think that?"

"Because she told me she'd met someone else and that this other person is the reason you two split up." Ms. Lancaster said. "Some girl. I think she's lying though. She's called a few times in the past several days and she says something different every time." That bitch! Raven thought, couldn't even tell her own mother the truth. She wouldn't have gone any damn where if Raven hadn't thrown her out. Hell, if she hadn't caught her with.... that's it! It must be!

"Thank you Mrs. Lancaster. You've been very helpful," Raven said quickly.

"Raven?" The woman said carefully. It surprised her, she couldn't remember Andi's mother ever saying her name before.

"Yes?"

"Do you think you could stop by sometime?" She asked. Raven was shocked into silence. When she didn't respond, the woman continued. "I know that we, you and I, haven't gotten on very well but I think there are some things you should know. Things about Andi." Raven was at a complete loss for words. She couldn't believe that after all this time Mrs. Lancaster would invite her into her home.

"Okay," was all she could say?

"Soon. And if you find her, tell her that she can come home only if she stops being so nasty and dates men. Dating your own kind is unnatural, against God," Mrs. Lancaster finished and hung up. Raven shook her head. She should have known that the woman wouldn't get off the phone without saying something insulting. Johni was looking at Raven, waiting for some answers.

"Well, what did she say?" Johni finally asked. Raven recounted the conversation and shared her suspicions with Johni.

"She didn't know where she was but I think I figured it

out by some of the things she said," Raven answered.

"Where?"

"Lee's," Raven answered.

"Lee? Who is that?"

"She's my ex-friend. Remember, the one I caught Andi with." Johni nodded. She remembered the one that she herself had wanted to kill for hurting Raven.

"Why would she go there?" Johni asked.

"Nowhere else to go," Raven answered. "All of our friends would side with me. Lee would be right there with her putting me down. Andi would have the support she needed. Besides Lee is a not-so-honest person herself. Andi could go to her and Lee would help her just to spite me."

"What do you do to these women?" Johni asked but before Raven could answer she held up her hand. "Nope, that's okay, after last night I have the answer to my own question," Raven laughed and kissed Johni.

"You know you ought to quit," Raven said kissing her again. Johni smiled.

"So what now?" Johni asked. Raven considered for a moment.

"Well if Andi is staying at Lee's she certainly isn't going to admit to it if we call. We'll need to go to Lee's to catch up with her," Raven said. The idea intrigued her. She loved the idea of seeing the two of them together again since Lee had led on like what happened that day in the house happened just to prove something to her. Johni saw the look in Raven's eyes and laughed.

"Thinking about catching people in the act?"

"Yep," Raven said and then laughed herself.

"So when do we go?" Raven looked at the clock, 1:00pm.

"Well now is as good a time as ever," she answered.

"Well then, let's go," Johni, said getting up. Raven smiled. She really loved this woman. For the first time in a long time she felt safe.

* * *

Andi watched them leave crouched down in the front seat of her rental car. She didn't stop to think about where they might be going. She didn't care. She needed a chance to get back into the house, and here it was handed to her on a silver platter. She waited ten minutes before she got out of the car and crossed the street. She kept a watchful eye out for anyone who might notice her. No one paid her any mind. She didn't figure they would because she had lived here too. In the time they had spent on this block she and Raven had never been particularly friendly with the neighbors. They kept to themselves just as everyone else on the block had. At the front door she turned for one more look up the block and then let herself in. The house smelled different. At first she wasn't sure what the difference was but as she moved down the hallway towards the bedroom she realized what it was. Andrews must wear men's cologne. So she thinks she's a man, does she, Andi thought as she reached the bedroom door.

"Then she won't be surprised when I rip her dick off," she whispered smiling. In the bedroom the smell was even stronger and served to fuel a rage within Andi.

"She's been in here," came the voice in her head, "in here fucking YOUR woman." Andi shook her head wildly. She didn't have time for this right now.

"Daddy, go away," she said to the air around her.

"In your bed, with your girl. Eating your pussy. Eating Raven's pussy. She's putting her tongue where yours should rightfully be," The voice mocked. Andi started to perspire. Beads of sweat ran down the sides of her face as she tried to will the voice into submission. She stood staring at the bed as the voice continued. "Can't help that now though, no siree bob! Now you've got to kill 'em both. Cut the dykes throat and bite off cute little Raven's pearl. Bite it off and swallow it. That's the only way no one else is going to get it." Andi was losing it. She could feel herself slipping. She searched her consciousness for reality. She mentally pushed at the voice to get it out of her head.

"Leave me alone!" She shouted, "I have work to do!

Leave me alone!" She was breathing hard now, on the edge of hyperventilation. Inside her head, laughter mocked her. Then another sound invaded her day mare. The front door slammed.

"Anybody home?!" Came a woman's voice. Andi didn't recognize the voice. She walked to the door and peered out. There, standing in the foyer, was a blond woman. Someone she had never seen before.

"Anybody home?" She called out again. "The door was open so I helped myself in. Johni, you here?" It was one of Andrews' friends. Andi smiled. Talk about wrong place, wrong time. She straightened her clothes and hair using the mirror next to the bedroom door. Andrews fucked with me, Andi thought, so I'll fuck with her. Taking a deep breath Andi smiled and stepped out into the hallway.

* * *

It had been a long time since Raven had been to Lee's. She went over once last year when Andi had insisted that they attend a party Lee was throwing. Looking back she should have known something was up then. They had spent far too much time huddled together in a corner, drinking beer and talking. That's the way it usually happened though. She was the last to know.

Johni had been quiet on the way over. Raven had left her alone with her thoughts but now she couldn't handle it anymore.

"Something bothering you?" Raven asked carefully. She realized that their relationship was really too young for Johni to be weathering things like this, but she knew that in reality it couldn't be helped. Still, she wanted to tread softly.

"Just thinking. About Andi and the way she is."

"What do you mean?" Raven prodded.

"Well, it's just hard to believe that someone you would chose to spend time with would be so mean," Johni answered. Uh oh, Raven thought.

"Someone I'd choose to be with? What do you mean?"

"You seem like a pretty good judge of character. I was surprised that something like this could sneak up on you," Johni said. Raven couldn't deny that. She really had been very surprised when Andi had changed within the first year of their relationship. She knew that Andi was an angry person inside but she'd had a hard time believing that she wouldn't change. That was why Raven wanted to talk to her. She needed a reason. She needed Andi to make some sense of all this. Raven refused to believe that she just overlooked the kind of person Andi really was been. Maybe something had been going on that Raven hadn't been aware of.

"Usually I'm a pretty good judge of character but this time I was swindled," Raven admitted. She hated saying that but she really had nowhere else to go on this one. "I just wanted to help her and I guess she took advantage of my nature." Johni reached over and grabbed Raven's hand. Raven was grateful.

"It's okay, it happens to the best of us," Johni said quietly. Raven felt better. She pulled off the road just shy of the housing complex. They had driven to the west side of Seattle. It wasn't a bad neighborhood, but it wasn't Raven's kind of neighborhood either, sort of lower middle class. Raven had changed a lot since they separated and this was just one of many changes.

"Is this it?" Johni asked looking around. It was not what she had expected.

"This is the area. Lee's house is two blocks that way," Raven said pointing east. "Hopefully she won't be home and Andi will be there by herself."

"Why?" Johni asked.

"Because Lee can be really difficult at times," Raven answered.

"What do you mean difficult?" Johni asked surveying her hand. She didn't want to get into a scuffle and not be able to handle her own.

"She's not a physical person but she can run her mouth and she's not beyond taking a punch now and again."

"Well, that's okay, I can handle that," Johni offered. Raven recognized the ego play and was tickled by it. Johni sat up a little straighter. Men, Raven thought to herself and had to smile.

"What's so funny?" Johni asked.

"Nothing," Raven said, "I just love you so much."

"I love you too," Johni said as she squeezed Raven's hand again. The familiar feeling of safety returned once again. "Now what?"

"Well," Raven said thoughtfully. "I guess we'd better walk up. We don't want to tip her off." Johni laughed.

"Look at you," Johni said hardly able to control her laughter.

"What?"

"You are in your element," Johni answered. Raven swiped at her.

"Very funny. I guess I watch a lot of TV," Raven laughed.

"I guess you do."

"Well," Raven pretended to pout. "Do you have any better ideas?"

"No, I think your idea is fine. I just had to laugh that's all." Raven took another swipe at Johni.

"You need to quit," she said laughing. They got out of the car and headed down the street. Johni took two steps and then mock tip toed.

"Stop it, Johni," Raven said sternly trying not to laugh. Johni stopped and laughed. Raven was amazed that they were actually having a good time in what should have otherwise been a bad situation. She watched Johni as they walked along. The confidence with which she walked was a real turn on for Raven. She smiled.

"What are you looking at?" Johni asked not looking over. Raven wasn't aware that Johni realized she was checking her out.

"You," Raven answered.

"You like what you see?"

"Yes."

"Good," Johni answered. Sure is cocky, Raven thought to herself. A moment later they were within view of Lee's house.

* * *

"Hi, can I help you?" Andi asked with her best smile. She had to do this right. The blond looked confused for a moment. Andi knew it was because she had never seen her before.

"Who are you?" The stranger asked.

"Oh, I'm sorry," Andi said offering her hand, "I'm Andi, a friend of Raven and Johni's. I'm staying a couple of days with them. And you are..."

"Brenda, Johni's ex-wife," the woman answered. She finally smiled. Andi sized her up quickly. She was small and probably not very strong. She had the appearance of one of those chicks with a lot of money that did nothing but spend it. "Would you happen to know where they are?" Andi smiled. "You've got her," said the voice in her head.

"Yes, as a matter-of-fact, I do. I was just on my way there."

"Good," the blond responded looking around absently, "maybe I can follow you."

"No problem," Andi said walking past Brenda and opening the front door. "Would you like to follow me?"

"Yes I would," she said trailing Andi out the door. "Thank you very much. Andi walked across the street and got into her rental. She couldn't believe how easy this was. These days people just trusted anyone. She made a U-turn in the street and glanced back to make sure the woman had gotten behind her. She had. With a wave Andi pulled off with Brenda, unsuspectingly, in tow.

* * *

"That's her house there," Raven said pointing, "the blue one." As far as Raven could see Lee's car was not there. That was not to say that it wasn't in the garage. The house wasn't a big one. Three bedrooms if Raven recalled correctly. Lee didn't have a dog.

"So what are we waiting for?" Johni asked.

"Nothing I suppose. Let's go," They walked up on the side of the yard so they wouldn't be seen by anyone inside. When they reached the door Johni knocked lightly. Raven stood off to the side so that if anyone looked through the peephole they wouldn't see her. No one answered immediately. Just as they were about to give up the door opened slightly.

"Yes?" It sounded like Lee. Raven thought she recognized her voice although the person behind the door didn't open it wide enough to see in.

"We're looking for Andi," Johni said.

"Andi who?" The person inside responded.

"Are you the person that lives here?"

"No, she's at work."

"Are you her roommate?" Johni asked.

"I'm a friend. Who are you?" Raven couldn't stand it anymore; she burst forward from the side of the porch catching everyone, including Johni off guard. The person in the door tried to shut it quickly but Raven had been too fast for her. Raven shoved the door inward.

"What the hell?!" The person inside yelled. Raven was on it though. She stepped through the door and confronted the person inside.

"I want to talk to you!" Just as she got it out Raven realized that the person she was facing was not Lee at all. She recovered quickly. "Where's Andi?!" The woman in the doorway looked baffled.

"And who the hell are you?!" Raven thought carefully

before proceeding. If Andi wasn't here Raven didn't want this woman to tip her off that they had been here.

"Is Andi Landcaster here?" Raven persisted.

"No."

"Is this 1762 Blossom Hill?" Raven asked trying to look as confused as she dared; all the while hoping that Johni was picking up her lead.

"No, this is 1712," the woman answered annoyed. Raven feigned embarrassment.

"Oh my," she said turning to Johni. "Gina! We've got the wrong house!" Johni threw her hands up in the air.

"I told you that if you went off halfcocked about that man things were going to get stupid!" Raven followed her lead.

"Oh.... I...am...so...sorry," Raven said to the woman in the doorway who was now looking rather amused. "I'm so embarrassed. What can I do to make this right? He left last night you see, and I didn't know, well, I hadn't any idea, oh damn..." Raven broke into tears. The woman became instantly comforting.

"It's okay. I understand that it was a mistake," she said putting a hand on Raven's shoulder and looking at Johni who rolled her eyes and shrugged her shoulders. "Maybe this guys no good," she offered. Raven just cried. Johni stepped up and put an arm around Raven's shoulder.

"There, there now, it'll be okay. I told you if you just

leave things alone he'll come back," Johni soothed. "I'm very sorry for the trouble," she said turning to the woman. "I'll take her home now. Thank you for being so understanding." The woman just shook her head. Johni and Raven left with her standing there feeling sorry for Raven and her imaginary run away husband/boyfriend. When they got around the block they both cracked up.

"I couldn't believe you back there," Johni said laughing. "You missed your calling."

"Hey you didn't do so bad yourself," Raven chimed in. "I am so glad you picked up on what I was trying to do."

"Why didn't you want her to know what was really going on? Lee still might have known where Andi was," Johni asked.

"If Lee knows where Andi is she wouldn't have told us. I don't want her alerting Andi if she does come over," Raven answered. "Lee has obviously found another play thing and that woman didn't appear to know who the hell Andi was."

"Oh, okay that makes sense. Now what?"

"Well, the only other thing I can think to do is go see Andi's mother." Raven said thoughtfully.

"Her mother? Why?"

"Maybe she can tell us something about where to find her. Hell, at the least we'll leave the bill and Andi's things with her."

"Well then, shall we go?" Johni asked bowing down. She just wanted Andi out of their lives.

"We shall," Raven answered bowing back. Raven took her hand and they walked back to the car. Raven's mind was going a hundred miles an hour about what she would say to Andi's mother.

* * *

Andi pulled into the parking lot of the hotel she'd been staying at. So far Brenda didn't suspect a thing. She got out and waited by her car while Brenda parked hers. Andi scanned the lot to make sure no one had noticed them. Brenda got out of her car, carefully locked the door, and joined Andi at hers.

"What are they doing here?" She questioned. For a second Andi saw suspicion setting in. Andi had to think fast.

"They came here for kind of a honeymoon." Andi offered. Instantly there was a new look in Brenda's eyes. Andi knew she had pushed the right button.

"What room?" Brenda asked, the anger apparent in her voice.

"167, in the back. Come on I'll take you." Andi said walking in the direction she had indicated. Behind her, Brenda fell into step without hesitation. Andi smiled.

* * *

Johni and Raven walked into the house and stopped to hug each other just inside the door. Being lesbians and in public didn't afford them the chance to be affectionate outside the house. Raven lifted her face and kissed Johni.

"You'll go with me to talk to Andi's mother, right?" She asked already knowing the answer.

"Now you know I will," Johni answered with a smile. Raven snuggled into her.

"I know, I just wanted to hear you say it," she cooed. Johni laughed and hugged her closer. After a couple of seconds she laughed again. Raven looked up at her.

"What's so funny?"

"Well, it's the strangest thing, I could have sworn I smelled Brenda's perfume in here," she answered thoughtfully.

"Oh you could?" Raven asked sarcastically, "Are we missing her?"

"No," Johni defended. Raven kissed Johni's neck.

"Well, just to make sure, let me show you a couple of good reasons why you should completely forget that woman." Raven started kissing Johni who was suddenly aroused.

"Brenda who?" Johni asked as they slowly made their way to the bedroom. Raven laughed quietly.

"So where are they?" Brenda asked. Andi had let her in and shut the door behind her. Brenda was now standing in the middle of Andi's dingy little room starting to get angry. Andi slipped her hand into her pocket and retrieved her knife.

"Well?" Brenda asked turning to face Andi. Andi smiled at her and the anger on Brenda's face suddenly slipped away. Nervousness was slowly setting in. Not so sure this was a good idea anymore eh Missy? Andi thought. Her smile broadened. She knew that to Brenda she was probably looking a little nuts but she couldn't help herself. She was just too pleased to have the opportunity to kill again. Brenda took a step backwards but before she could take another, Andi was on her. She grabbed her and shoved her onto the bed. Brenda started to scream and fight but Andi quickly shoved the knife against her throat.

"If you make one more sound I'll just cut your throat and that will be that," Andi whispered. "I will be greatly disappointed to have to do that." Brenda's eyes widened as realization set in. She had followed a lunatic to this hotel room. Andi could see these thoughts in her eyes.

"Yep, that's right. Certifiable and proud of it!" Andi sung out. Brenda looked around wildly. "Forget it babe, you're here for the duration. No way out." Tears welled up in Brenda's eyes.

"Why," was all she could squeak out?

"Why," Andi laughed. She climbed on top of Brenda, straddled her and put her face in Brenda's. "You, my dear, were at the wrong place, at the WRONG time." Andi started laughing and Brenda cried harder. Andi reached over and pulled a pillowcase off one of the two pillows. Not moving from her position, she used her knife as she stayed on top of Brenda to shred the case. Brenda took this opportunity to buck upwards but Andi just sat more squarely on top of her. Brenda whined as Andi grabbed her hands. She fought against her but Andi was too strong and overtook her easily. In no time Andi had Brenda's arms tied to the headboard of the bed. Brenda continued to cry. Every time she attempted to make a loud noise Andi would stop long enough to return the knife to her throat.

"If you will bear with me for just a little while," Andi told her, "I might let you go." Andi continued her work. She worked diligently and quickly. When she was finished she stood back to admire her handiwork. She had tied Brenda to the bed with her arms tied together at the headboard and her legs tied spread eagle at the foot of the bed. Brenda looked horrified and about to scream. Andi gagged her with the last of the pillowcase. Tears streamed down her face and the terror in her eyes spurred Andi on. "Tell me something, Brenda," Andi said sitting next to her on the bed. Brenda tried to move away but the ties wouldn't give. "Is Johni a good fuck? She'd have to be a tremendously good fuck because that's the only reason I can think of that Raven would want her." Brenda's eyes widened. "Is she Brenda? Is Johni Andrews a good FUCK," she bellowed in Brenda's face. Brenda nodded her head yes. Andi jumped backwards as though she'd gotten an electrical shock. "I knew it! I knew it! She'd have to be, that's the only answer." Andi started pacing the room. She was sweating hard now and her heart was pounding with anger. She favored Brenda with a glance and then went back to pacing, trying to decide what to do. Suddenly the voice was back.

"Fuck her."

"What? What are you talking about?" Andi said to the air. Brenda's eyes widened.

"Fuck her," the voice offered again. "She said Andrews was a good fuck. Show her what a good fuck really is." Andi looked at Brenda.

"You've got a point." Andi answered.

"Of course I do. This little bitch said that Andrews was good. Some nerve eh? How the hell does she know? She's never had you," the voice egged on. Andi laughed. That was true. How could this bitch know? Okay, Andi thought, okay. She walked to the end of the bed. She was still holding her pocketknife in her right hand. She cut away

Brenda's clothes with the knife. Brenda whined the entire time. Andi hated that. Why did they always whine? They want you to be aggressive but then when you are they complain. Women! Naked, Brenda started to cry harder. Andi removed her own clothes very calmly. Once in a while she would steal a glance at the woman tied to the bed. Not a bad body. Too bad, she thought. Undressed, Andi stood at the foot of the bed. She took a deep breath and then crawled up the length of Brenda's body. The woman squirmed but couldn't get away. They both knew that. Andi smiled.

"Not a bad little bod," she cooed. Andi kissed Brenda on the forehead. Brenda made a retching noise.

"I wouldn't throw up right now if I were you, baby, you'll drown." Andi offered. Brenda half-heartedly squirmed again. "A fighter. I like fighters," Andi said as she ran her finger over Brenda's nipples. She pinched the right one between her fingers. Brenda jumped indicating that it hurt. "Did that hurt?" Andi asked sarcastically. "Here let me fix that for you." Andi got up on her knees and grabbed Brenda's nipple in her fingers again. With her right hand she put her knife at the base of the nipple. "You didn't need these anyway," She said and she sliced into Brenda's skin. At first it was tough but once the first slice was made the knife slid through like butter. Brenda screamed through the gag.

"Now see, that didn't hurt so bad, did it?" Andi asked sitting back to look at her handy work. Blood was gushing from the wound where Brenda's nipple was just seconds before.

"Aw, look, you're uneven. Let me fix that," Andi offered as she sliced the left nipple off as well. Brenda was screaming so hard now that Andi was sure she would pass out. Her face was red and her eyes were bloodshot, threatening to bulge out of her head. To Andi it looked almost comical. Andi lay back down next to Brenda. "Now, you want to see what real fucking is all about?" Andi asked in Brenda's ear. Bringing the knife down the length of Brenda's stomach Andi stopped at her crotch. Brenda suddenly got quiet. Her eyes widened with horror. Andi played the knife along the crease between Brenda's legs. Quietly she started crying again. It was not a terrified cry as before but more a wailing, like a woman whose child has just been killed by a car. "Do I turn you on, Brenda?" Andi asked calmly. "You think Johni Andrews is a good fuck? Here let me show you what it's like to really get fucked," Andi whispered. She rose up and plunged the knife into Brenda's vagina.

Chapter 20

They left around five for Andi's mother's house. Raven felt strange going but she wanted to get rid of Andi's things and be shed of her responsibility to her. The house was on the Upper East Side and was in an obviously well to do neighborhood. Johni let out a low whistle.

"Nice digs."

"It's all right," Raven responded. She was not about to admit that she was impressed, although she was. Raven pulled the MG around and parked at the curb.

"Ready?" Johni asked reaching over and tapping her arm. Raven let out a long sigh.

"I guess," she answered. They got out and grabbed the few things from the car that were Andi's. Raven led the way to the door. She pushed the doorbell and stepped back. After a few moments the porch light came on. Dusk was just creeping in but for some people flipping the porch light on was just a habit. Raven had even done it in the middle of the day once or twice. The door opened slowly.

"Can I help you," came a voice on the other side of the screen. The voice sounded frail.

"It's Raven Michaels, Mrs. Lancaster, Andi's ex-girlfriend." After a moment the screen door opened.

"Come in," the woman said backing up. Raven stepped

through the door followed closely by Johni. Once inside the woman closed the door. "Go into the living room and sit down," she insisted. Raven and Johni did as they were told. Raven took this time to look around. She had never been here before and it wasn't at all what she had imagined. She had pictured a dungeon looking place. This was actually quite nice. The place was decorated in pastels and antique furniture. It looked old fashion but it was nice. Raven felt almost comfortable. They went into the living room and sat down on the couch. After a few minutes Mrs. Lancaster joined them with a tray of glasses and some sodas. She offered them both one and then took a seat across from them.

"Mrs. Lancaster, this is Johni Andrews, a friend of mine," Raven offered.

"Johni Andrews, the author?" Mrs. Lancaster asked.

"Yes ma'am," Johni answered. The woman looked impressed. "I was sorry to hear about your accident," Mrs. Lancaster offered. "How are you doing?" Raven was touched.

"I'm much better now, thank you," Johni answered. Andi's mother nodded her head.

"Good, such a horrible thing, the accident and all. I don't know why people drink and drive. It's a shame," she added. Both Raven and Johni nodded their heads in agreement.

"Mrs. Lancaster? We brought some of Andi's things to you. I hope it's not an inconvenience but I needed to clear out her stuff. There's also a bill that she needs to get." Raven hoped it was okay, just bringing this stuff without calling first. "We have tried to find her but she doesn't seem to be anywhere around. We were hoping you didn't mind."

"No, not at all. Sooner or later she'll come by and she can get her stuff then," she said waving her hand in the air. Raven was relieved.

"Mrs. Lancaster, you said there was a reason you wanted me to come by?" Raven prompted. She was starting to feel the need to leave. Andi's mother looked nervous.

"I needed to talk to someone about something that's bothering me and I figured since you knew Andi..." she started. Raven wasn't sure she wanted to be this woman's confidant. But whatever was bothering her was bothering her a lot.

"What is it?" Raven pushed. Mrs. Lancaster fidgeted and then got up. She paced.

"I don't want her to get mad at me. She's so mean when she's angry." Raven guessed that the woman was talking about Andi. She glanced over at Johni who looked just as confused as she was.

"Mrs. Lancaster what is it?" Raven prodded. Andi's

mother looked thoughtful for a moment and then the look on her face changed. She straightened up and looked Raven in the eye.

"Please leave," she said and turned towards the door. Raven and Johni looked at each other. Johni shrugged her shoulders.

"Mrs. Lancaster, I thought you had something to speak to me about," Raven said standing up. Andi's mother walked towards the door.

"You are mistaken," the woman answered. "If you'll leave Andi's things I'll see that she gets them." Raven and Johni walked to the door.

"Thank you Mrs. Lancaster," Raven said stepping out the door. Johni followed closely. When they were outside Raven turned back to the door. "If there's anything we can help..." The door slammed shut. Raven stood there looking at the door unbelieving. Johni shook her head and took Raven's arm.

"The woman is a fruitcake," Johni offered leading Raven to the car. Raven allowed her self to be lead but kept looking at the house. Once in the car she laughed.

"Was it me or were we talking to two different people in there?" She asked. Johni laughed with her.

"It wasn't you. I met them both too."

"Damn, what a weird family," Raven said starting the car.

"Takes all kinds," Johni agreed. "At least you're rid of Andi's things.

"That's true. Rid of her things and rid of her," Raven sung out. "Let's go home."

* * *

By the time she was finished, Andi had cleaned up the place so well that you'd never even guess anyone had been there. She wished she had been able to clean up the hotel room as well but, hell, she was in a hurry. She'd do it later. She was lucky enough to find Raven and her dyke gone again so she went back into the house to finish the business she'd started when Brenda the wonder-fuck had interrupted her. (She hadn't been so good; she bled all over the place.) Now that she was done leaving her calling cards she would leave. Dark was falling and she had other work to do. Slipping out the door, Andi carefully locked it behind her. She stood on the porch for a minute and took a deep breath. Damn it felt good to be alive. Whistling Andi went back to her car.

* * *

Raven and Johni stopped in town and got a hamburger. It was Johni's suggestion. Raven detested eating that way but to please Johni she had conceded. She had to admit though the hamburger from Rhino's drive-in was pretty good, if you didn't mind grease. No wonder Johni was so unhealthy. Raven made a mental note to watch her more carefully. After the burger they went home. Parking the MG in the driveway Raven switched off the lights and sat for a minute.

"What?" Johni asked. When Raven didn't move she decided to wait too.

"It is just so nice to come home and actually want to be here," she answered. "You don't know how many times I sat in this car, when Andi and I were together, and wished I didn't have to go in."

"I can imagine." Raven looked over at Johni and smiled.

"I love you."

"I love you too," Johni said smiling back. "You don't have to worry about Andi anymore. You're with me now."

"Thanks." Raven said rubbing Johni's arm.

"It's my job."

"Hey, you aren't tired," Raven noted happily.

"Didn't take the medicine again."

"Johni,"

"I forgot."

"Yeah sure," Raven said, "you need to quit." Johni smiled. Raven ran her hand through Johni's hair. "You ready to go in?"

"Come on," Johni answered. They got out of the car

and walked arm in arm into the house.

* * *

From across the street Andi watched as Raven and Johni walked into the house.

"Have a good evening ladies," Andi whispered. She started the car and headed for the hotel.

* * *

"Raven, are you coming to bed?" Johni yelled from the bedroom.

"In a minute," Raven answered. She was locking things up and she decided that she would do just one thing on her computer before she went to bed. She popped her head in the bedroom door. "I'll be there in a minute; I just want to check something."

"Better hurry," Johni called out. "I'm pretty tired."

"Okay," Raven called back. She went into the office and noticed right off that the computer screen was on. The protective plastic cover was still on it but underneath she could see the light from the saver. She didn't remember turning that back on. She stopped and took stock of the room. It didn't look like anyone else had been here. She walked over and sat down in her chair. Reaching over, Raven removed the cover. The screen saver was bright and what Raven saw on the screen horrified her. She gasped and pushed her chair back.

"Johni!" She cried out. Johni was there within seconds.

"What?! What's wrong?" Raven pointed to the computer screen. Johni felt her stomach heave a little. There, taped to the screen were pictures of a mutilated body. There was no way to tell who it was, the head had been removed but it was definitely the body of a female. The photographs, taken in several different positions, showed the mutilation. Raven turned towards Johni and buried her face in her shoulder.

"Johni, who would do this?"

"I don't know but we need to call the police," Johni said not able to take her eyes off the photos.

"I'll go," Raven said and started for the door. Something suddenly occurred to Johni.

"NO!" She shouted. Raven stopped in her tracks. "Stay here, let me look around." Raven didn't argue but she didn't stay either. She shadowed Johni every step of the way as she searched the house. When Johni was finally satisfied that no one else was in the house, she picked up the phone and called the police. Raven sat down on the couch.

"Are you okay?" Johni asked as she sat down next to Raven and put an arm around her. Raven nodded her head.

"I guess so. Who would do such a thing?"

"I don't know, but I'll tell you one thing, tomorrow the

locks get changed," Johni stated.

"I can do that," Raven said quietly.

"Excuse me?"

"I can do that, change the locks I mean." Johni looked impressed.

"What can't you do?" Raven smiled in spite of herself. Johni hugged her.

"Don't worry, everything's going to be all right," Johni reassured her. Raven looked up and smiled at Johni kissing her on the chin.

The police finally left around 11 o'clock. Raven and Johni fell into bed. The police hadn't been able to offer them anything other than to change the locks. There was no forced entry and no fingerprints. They took the pictures with them. Raven snuggled up under Johni.

"Are you okay?" Johni asked her for the fifth time tonight. Raven snuggled harder.

"Yes, I'm okay. It's just eerie that's all," Raven answered. Johni had to agree. She checked the house several times and finally, on the fourth round, was satisfied enough to go to bed. "Are we going to be all right, Johni?"

"Yes," Johni answered holding Raven tighter. "It was probably a prank. The blood on those pictures probably wasn't even real." She didn't believe that but she wanted Raven to feel safe. After the police had finished investigating, Johni walked outside with them. They didn't believe it was a prank either. The pictures showed what was obviously a woman, someone who had been killed, just before the pictures had been taken. Her nipples had been cut off and with all the blood between her legs; Johni would be willing to bet she'd been raped. This coupled with the fact that the body had no head, was more than unnerving. Whoever had done this was sick. Johni lay looking up at the ceiling. She felt Raven breathing evenly now. It hadn't taken her long to go to sleep at all. Johni wondered briefly if the person who left the pictures was the same person who had hit her. No, she decided that was crazy. Pushing the thought from her mind Johni feel asleep.

* * *

The clock glowed 2:15 a.m. Andi sat across the street again in the rental. She had driven by once earlier this evening and had seen the police cars. She found the pictures. Andi wondered if Johni recognized Brenda. She doubted it. Andi got out of her car and walked across to the house. The sound of an approaching car sent her diving into the bushes. A police cruiser passed slowly. Andi cursed herself for not having seen it. After it was out of sight, Andi headed for the house again.

Quietly Andi let herself in. She stood for a moment, listening for sounds. She heard none. Creeping towards the bedroom Andi stopped and peeked into the office just to reassure herself that the pictures had indeed gotten someone's attention. She tiptoed to the computer and flipped on the screen. She quietly typed a message and turned the screen off again. She giggled a little. She's going to be afraid to go near that computer, she thought. Andi left the office and continued to the bedroom. The figures in the bed didn't move. She felt rage start to well up inside her again but she quickly stifled it. She turned and made her way, in the dark, back towards the kitchen. Once there she opened the fridge and took out a soda. Making note of the contents, Andi closed the door and quickly went back to the car. She returned with a small sack. Opening the refrigerator, she dumped the contents of the bag onto the top shelf. She closed the door, smiling at her handiwork. That'll do, she thought. She headed for the front door. In the foyer she stopped at the large mirror on the wall. She looked at her own reflection and smiled.

"Perfect," she whispered. Andi left, locking the door behind her.

Chapter 21

Raven woke up at six o'clock. She was still tired but her internal clock wouldn't let her sleep any later. She moved to get up and Johni stirred. She didn't want to wake her up. How was she supposed to heal if she didn't get enough rest? Besides she had therapy today and she'd need her strength. She waited until Johni settled back into a deeper sleep and then eased her way out of bed. Padding quietly into the bathroom, she closed the door behind her so the shower wouldn't wake Johni. Raven stood in the shower for fifteen minutes trying to let the water wash away the tension she was feeling.

The pictures last night had unnerved her. How could someone be so evil? The realization that someone had been in the house was worse, in her house. She felt violated. Turning the off shower she toweled off and brushed her teeth. She then quietly snuck into the closet and put on her clothes. She went over and kissed Johni on the head before leaving the room. She thought about shutting the door but then thought twice. She didn't want to feel cut off from Johni. For a moment she considered going back to bed until Johni was ready to get up but she knew she was just being silly. Raven turned lights on as she went through the house. It was dawn outside but still too dark to leave the lights off. She headed for her office. She stopped when she remembered the clothes she'd left in the chair in the bedroom. She'd better put them away before she forgot. Going back to the bedroom Raven spent the next half hour folding and hanging clothes. She usually put off that task but she had noticed that Johni was neat and orderly. It was making Raven self-conscious. She vowed to try harder to pick up after herself. Finishing the clothes she headed back to the office. She was sitting at her desk this time when she remembered the clothes in the washer. Damn, she thought, I'm never going to get to work. She went to the laundry room and put the clothes in the dryer. By the time she came back in it was seven o'clock. Johni met her half way down the hall.

"Hey, I was looking for you," Johni said, gathering her up into her arms. Raven smiled.

"Well, I was trying to get at my computer before you woke up, but a hundred different things came up," Raven answered.

"Well, I'm going to get in the shower and I'll take my time if you want to try again," Johni offered.

"Great."

"Unless..." Johni teased, "You want to join me." Raven laughed.

"If you had it your way we'd never get anything done."

"Okay, okay, I'm out of here." Raven watched Johni go. She had a cute butt. She smiled and Johni turned and caught her looking.

"Caught you," Johni called out, going into the bedroom.

"Yeah, so what..." Raven yelled back. She heard Johni laughing as the shower came on. Raven went into the office.

"Finally," she said out loud. She sat at her desk, flipped on the screen and turned to get her file on Doug Bryant. (She was creating a system for him.) When she turned back around she stopped as her eyes focused on the monitor. The first thing that caught her eye was LOVE ME, LOVE YOU. There was a message on the screen signed love me, love you. The only person who could have written that message was Andi. She signed all her letters like that. That bitch had to have been in here recently. Did she still have a key? Raven was mad. She took the time to read the message and as she did her anger melted into fear and realization. There across her computer screen in bold letters read,

YOU NEVER KNOW WHAT SOMEONE MIGHT DO!!!!

LOVE ME, LOVE YOU

The pictures flashed through her mind but she refused to believe that Andi could be responsible for something so gruesome. Or could she? In the other room she heard the shower go off. Waiting a few minutes she went to get Johni. By the time she got into the room Johni was dressed.

"Hey, I need to show you something," Raven, said. Johni was instantly concerned.

"No more pictures of dead women I hope," Johni joked nervously. Raven didn't say anything, she just lead Johni into the office and pointed to the screen. Johni read the message and then looked at Raven.

"Who wrote that?" She asked knowing from the way Raven was reacting that she must have some idea.

"Andi," Raven answered.

"Are you sure?"

"Yes. Andi ended all of her letters with love you love me. It was something her father always said to her," Raven explained.

"So she's been in here? In the house."

"I think so."

"Recently," Johni said looking around.

"I worked on the computer yesterday and the message wasn't there," Raven said slowly, "so she had to have been in here..."

"Last night," Johni finished reaching for the phone. "I'm calling the police. This crazy bitch must have been in here while we were asleep." A shiver ran down Raven's spine and she hugged herself. The thought of Andi, or anybody, for that matter, being in the house while they were sleeping gave her the creeps. She listened as Johni called the police. When she hung up she reached for Raven and hugged her.

"Are you okay?" Raven nodded. "The police are sending someone over. Raven, I need to ask you something..." Johni said carefully. Raven interrupted her with a wave of her hand.

"I've already thought about it and I don't know. I'd like to think that Andi would never do anything like leaving those pictures. But based on the things she's done recently, hell, who knows."

"Does it seem like something she'd do?" Johni asked. "You know how some people can get when they feel like they've lost something they didn't want to give up."

"It doesn't seem like anything I could picture her doing," Raven said thoughtfully, "but there was something she said to me in the hospital cafeteria and on Reman's. Now that I think about it..."

"What?" Johni prodded. Raven looked up and Johni could see fear in her eyes.

"In the hospital she said she'd kill us both," Raven explained, "At the time I didn't take her seriously but now, looking back, she could have meant that. And on the Hill she said the same thing that's on the screen," Raven said indicating the computer screen.

"YOU NEVER KNOW WHAT SOMEONE MIGHT DO," Johni read again. She looked at Raven and watched her sit back down in her chair.

"Johni, what if she's who left the pictures? What if Andi has gone nuts?" she asked. Johni considered for a moment.

"People don't just go nuts Raven. You lived with this woman for four years. If she'd been mental you'd have picked up on it by now," Johni explained. "She's probably just pissed off and sneaked in here yesterday to leave this message."

"Why did you call the police then?" Raven asked. Johni chose her answer carefully.

"Just to be on the safe side, on the off chance that Andi isn't the one who left the message."

"She's the only one who could have," Raven said absently. She was staring at the computer screen. Johni didn't like seeing her worry.

"The police will be here any minute and we'll get this whole thing cleared up," Johni said squeezing Raven's shoulder. "Okay?"

"Okay," Raven said looking up at Johni. Her protector. What would I do without her? Raven thought. "I'm kind of hungry, are you?" Johni smiled at her.

"That's my girl. Yeah, as a matter of fact I am."

"Come on then. Let's eat something while we wait for the police," Raven said getting up and taking Johni's hand. Johni pulled her close.

"I love you," Johni whispered hugging her.

"I love you too," Raven said hugging her back. "Come on." Raven led Johni into the kitchen. "Why don't you sit while I see what I can find?" Johni smiled and took a seat at the table.

"You know, someday you are going to have to try my cooking," she said watching Raven get a large glass bowl from the cabinet.

"Yeah, someday," Raven said sarcastically. Johni laughed as she watched Raven reach for the refrigerator door. Raven turned and smiled at her as she opened the door, "Really, I'm sure you're a very good co...," Raven dropped the glass bowl and stepped back gasping. The bowl shattered as it hit the floor. Johni jumped from her chair.

"What? What's wrong Raven?" Johni asked rushing to her side. Raven couldn't do anything but point. Johni followed her finger. There, on the top shelf of the refrigerator, was the head of a cat. Blood was all over the shelf and although it was dried now, it was obvious that when the head had been placed in the refrigerator it had been a fresh kill.

"That's Bo, the cat from next door. We use, to, feed it, now and....then," Raven stammered. Johni let go of Raven and took a closer look. The head was severed at the base of the neck. The cut was clean. Whoever cut the cat's head off did it on purpose. Johni felt her stomach heave slightly. Behind her a sob escaped Raven. Johni turned and gathered Raven up into her arms leading her into the living room. Raven cried openly now. The sight of the head had been too much. Johni held her while she cried. After a couple of minutes Raven stopped and tried to regain her composure.

"I'm sorry," she said wiping her eyes, "I just can't believe anyone could be that cruel." Johni nodded in agreement. She had to admit; whoever did this was a few bricks short of a load. The doorbell rang and Raven jumped.

"It's okay," Johni soothed, "It's probably the cops." She got up and went to the door. It was indeed the police. While Raven stayed on the couch, Johni took them in and showed them, first the message and then the head. Afterwards they all sat down in the living room and discussed Raven's suspicions.

"Why do you think your ex-roommate had anything to do with this Ms. Michaels?" One of the officers asked.

"She always signed all her letters with that phrase," Raven answered.

"Do you have anything that you could show us that she signed that way?"

"No, I don't," Raven, said thoughtfully. She had gotten rid of all Andi's things as well as the letters she'd written to her. "I have no reason to lie."

"No ma'am," the officer continued, "I don't believe you do but what we have here is only hearsay and we can't pursue this without hard evidence." Raven blinked at the officer in disbelief.

"You mean because she hasn't actually signed her name to any of this you can't do anything about it?"

"We ran a check on Ms. Lancaster and there's nothing on her. Right now we have nothing indicating that she's involved," the officer defended.

"But what about the message and the neighbor's cat," Raven asked?

"The only thing we have is a horrible prank and a message on a computer screen that could have come from anywhere. Hardly reason to suspect anyone. We'll check out Ms. Lancaster's whereabouts but other than that our hands are tied," The officer said getting to his feet. Raven stood also, shaking her head.

"When she actually kills one of us, then can you do anything?" She asked sarcastically. Johni put a hand on Raven's shoulder.

"We'll have a patrol car come by once in a while. In the meantime, change your locks and give us a call if anything else turns up," The officer offered stepping out the front door.

"Call you for what?" Raven mumbled under her breath.

Johni squeezed her shoulder and Raven shut-up.

"Thank you officers," Johni said shutting the door. Raven was pissed. She marched back into the living room and started to pace. Johni sat on the arm of the sofa and watched her.

"Call them, for what?! They can't do anything," she said as she paced. "What if she comes in next time and kills us both? Then what?"

"Raven, they don't have anything on her," Johni said watching her continue to pace. "It's not like she has a criminal record or anything." Raven stopped pacing and faced Johni

"What if she does," Raven offered. "What if whatever her mother had to tell us has something to do with this? She wanted to tell me something awfully bad." Johni considered it. She had to agree with Raven. The woman did seem upset.

"So what are you going to do? Her mother decided not to talk to you." Johni pushed. Raven thought for a minute. Johni was right.

"She has to talk to us. If she knows anything that could help us prove that Andi is behind this we need to know," Raven said pacing again. Johni watched as Raven walked the length of the room and then back again.

"What makes you so sure it's Andi?" Johni asked. "This morning you said you didn't think she'd do anything like this." Raven stopped and turned to Johni.

"Because she hated that cat," Raven answered quietly, "and because she always said she wanted to cut its head off.

* * *

Andi stormed into the room.

"Fuck, fuck, fuck!" She bellowed. She'd gone to see her mother and the damn police were there. "Fuck!" She shouted again. She thought she'd have time. She needed to get to dear old mom this morning before the cops did. Eight fucking a.m. in the morning! Shit, she thought, Raven must have woke up early. Andi glanced around the room. It was a mess. Brenda's corpse was still sprawled across the bed and her head sat on the table by the window. Andi sat in the chair next to the table and turned Brenda's head around so she could see the face.

"Can you fucking believe this?" She asked the head. "I really thought I'd have enough time! I swear Raven can't sleep in for shit. I'll bet old steel-fuck Andrews doesn't get up at dawn. It had to be Raven." Andi looked at the head and then at the corpse on the bed and smiled. "Guess you weren't up early," she said laughing. Andi got up and went into the bathroom. Looking in the mirror she studied her own eyes. "Do I look crazy, Brenda," she called out. "I don't feel crazy." Andi tried to stare her own reflection down. After a few moments she turned back to the severed head. "Now I'm really in a pickle, Brenda. Now I have to figure out how to get into mommy's house before the cops ransack my room there." Andi walked over and sat on the foot of the bed. "My diaries are there, not a good thing," she said slapping the corpse on the leg, "not a good thing at all." She really had figured on going by her mother's at eight and being out of there by the time the police stopped by. Andi knew they wouldn't have anything on her but she also realized that Raven would insist they follow up her suspicions that Andi had left her those little surprises.

"Raven," she said addressing the head again. "Did you meet her? Smart little bitch." Andi walked over and sat in the chair again. She put a hand on the top of Brenda's head. "Now there's a good fuck." Andi laughed and patted the top of the head. "What to do, what to do..." Andi chimed. Her stomach growled loudly. She realized she hadn't eaten anything in a while. "Brenda, I'm going out for some chow. Want anything?" Andi asked getting up. She walked to the door and turned around surveying the room again. The maid is going to be pissed, she thought. "Guess you're not hungry, huh," she said to the head. "Oh well, more for me," she said laughing. Andi left and locked the door behind her. The "DO NOT DISTURB" sign swung carelessly on the knob.

Chapter 22

Raven and Johni again found themselves standing on the walk in front of Andi's mother's house.

"I still don't think she'll talk to us," Johni said looking up and down the block.

"She will," Raven, said stepping forward, "she'll have no choice." They'd talked for a long time about what to do next. Raven knew it was Andi who was getting into the house. She could just feel it. The message on the computer told her so and the cat's head in the refrigerator confirmed it. Andi was nuts and on the loose. Raven was still having a hard time with the concept. They had lived together for four years and she had never seen any indication that Andi might have serious problems. Sure, sometimes the way she spoke made Raven cringe but it was only talk. She never considered that Andi would actually follow through with some of her crazy notions. She desperately needed one of two things, to either prove her suspicions or disprove them. In her heart she actually hoped to disprove them. They walked to the door and Johni rang the doorbell. After a few moments the door cracked slightly.

"Yes?" A voice asked.

"Mrs. Lancaster? It's Raven Michaels. I need to ask you a few questions.

"May we come in?" For a few seconds Raven didn't

think she'd let them in but suddenly the screen door swung slowly outward.

"Come in already, you're letting out my heat." Johni and Raven went inside.

The house was indeed warm. Mrs. Lancaster led them into the living room. This time she offered no refreshments, only a place to sit. She appeared nervous to Raven,.

"Mrs. Lancaster," Raven started, "we need to know if you have any idea at all where Andi might be." The woman shifted in her seat.

"The police were here this morning you know. They said they needed to ask Andi some questions. Did you send them?" The woman demanded. Raven was starting to feel that Johni was right. Maybe Andi's mother wouldn't be of any help at all.

"Yes, Mrs. Lancaster, they came because of something that happened at our home. Do you know where Andi is?" Raven asked again. Andi's mother got up from her seat and walked to the window. As she did her face changed so drastically that both Johni and Raven saw the change.

"She's no good you know," the woman spat out. "She was a Daddy's girl and he was a freak. He was nuts and so is she!" Raven was taken aback. The hatred in the woman's eyes was fire-fed. Whatever she felt at this moment for Andi was intense. Raven looked at Johni who indicated that she should prod the woman.

"Mrs. Lancaster, can you tell me what you mean? Andi might be trying to hurt me and if there's something wrong with her I need to know," Raven said quietly. She didn't want to upset the woman. She needed to know what she was talking about.

"Hurt you?" The woman laughed. "She wouldn't be trying to hurt you, she'd be trying to kill you." She continued to laugh as Raven's mouth dropped open. Were they talking about the same woman?

"I don't think I understand," Raven started. Suddenly Mrs. Lancaster left the room. Raven and Johni looked inquisitively at one another.

"What's going on?" Johni whispered. Raven tried to see where the woman went.

"I don't know," Raven answered, "but it keeps getting stranger and stranger." Mrs. Lancaster came back into the room with a box, which she promptly dropped into Johni's lap. Johni jumped slightly and looked at Raven.

"What's this?" Raven asked peering into the box.

"Her books!" The older woman said walking back to the window. "Now take them and leave before she changes her mind." Raven looked perplexed.

"She? She who," Raven asked?

"GO!" The woman bellowed. Johni and Raven scrambled to their feet and headed for the door. "GET

OUT AND DON'T COME BACK!" Johni opened the front door and Raven practically ran over her trying to get out the door. At the car they finally stopped and looked back at the house. Johni shook her head.

"Don't have to tell me twice. Geez!"

"I hear ya," Raven said. "Come on; let's go see what's in this box." They climbed into the car and headed for home.

* * *

Andi ate at Jack In The Box and went back to the hotel. She unlocked the door and stepped into darkness.

"Honey, I'm home," she bellowed. Flipping on the light by the bed, Andi walked over and kissed Brenda's severed head. "And how was your day?" She sat down in the chair and stared at the corpse. Too bad she's dead, Andi thought; I could use some pussy right about now. Oh well, her loss. Andi got up and went into the bathroom. She peeled her clothes off and turned on the shower. While the water warmed she stood in the mirror. Her reflection waned for a moment. When it returned her father was standing behind her. He still had those same clothes on, he really should change em, she thought, the blood on them is already dried. Going to be a bitch to get out.

"Hi Daddy," Andi said smiling. He father smiled back at her.

"Hey Andi-pandy! What's doin's?" Her father asked.

"Nothin, gonna take a shower," Andi answered. Her father leered at her in the mirror.

"Can I come?" He asked. Andi frowned at the reflection.

"I told you I wasn't doing that no more!" Andi stated coolly. Her father smiled.

"Oh yeah, you're a l-e-s-b-i-a-n!" He mocked. Andi furrowed her brow.

"And so..." she asked starting to get angry.

"And....so you eat pussy that's what! But who showed you how, huh, who showed you how to do it right?"

"You did," Andi answered sheepishly.

"That's right, and don't you forget it, ya hear!" he bellowed.

"Yes sir," Andi answered. Her father laughed and Andi turned and stepped into the shower. As she did he disappeared from the mirror. "I won't forget Daddy, no siree-bob."

* * *

"She is certifiable," Johni said shaking her head. Raven looked up and then back to the book she had in her hand. She had to agree. She had lived with a lunatic for four years and didn't have a clue. They had come home and dumped the books on the bed. She and Johni spent the better part off three hours reading through what turned out to be Andi's personal diaries. It was incredible. The books, seven in all, detailed the killings of at least nine animals and eight people including her own father. If what's written in these books was true then Andi's father had died at her hands after years of sexual abuse and terror.

Andi's diaries dated back seventeen years to when she was a small child. She talked about her father and his abuse, her mother and her mental problems and the "experiments" she started doing on small animals when she was eight, slowly working her way up to human beings. Andi wanted to understand pain by inflicting it on something or someone else. She was sick. Putting the last book down Raven shook her head as tears welled up in her eyes.

"I had no idea," she said looking up at Johni. She reached out and touched Johni's hand. "I really didn't have a clue." Johni nodded.

"She hid it well," Johni offered. Raven sat on the edge of the bed and wondered how she could have missed all this. They lived together, ate together, my God, she thought, I had a relationship with this woman!" As if she had read her mind Johni got off the bed and came around to sit next to her.

"A lot of people live together and never really know

each other," she offered, "we see only what we want to see, if you really think about it." Raven nodded. She was numb from all the revelations she was discovering. One of the books slid off the bed and hit the floor. Raven bent over and picked it up. Something under the bed caught her eye. She reached down and came up with yet another leather bound book like the ones on the bed. It was dated in sequence with the rest of them. This one was dated the year she and Andi had gotten together. Opening the book Raven started to read. What she found in this book was quite different from the others. In this book there were no violent dreams or killings. Only happy memories of the two of them with only an occasional hint of the sickness Andi had written in the other books. Raven flipped through the book further and found the final entry. It was dated the same day as Johni's accident.

I did it. I drove that dyke right off over the edge. She deserved it. Raven is mine and I'll be fucked if some dyke bitch is going to come along and take her. Should have seen her face. I could have busted a gut I laughed so hard. Raven will be home soon. When she hears that the dyke is dead she'll leave well enough alone. It's a good thing because if by some chance she survived I'll have to kill 'em both. It would be hard to kill my Raven too but I would. I'd have too. I'll show Raven who's in control. She'll wish she never met that dyke.

Raven was in shock. Andi had run Johni off the road on purpose. It hadn't been a drunk after all. She handed the book to Johni, indicated the passage, and let her read it. While Johni read, Raven went to the bathroom and threw up. When she was done, she emerged from the bathroom to find Johni shaking her head.

"This is incredible," Johni said as Raven sat back down.

"She's got to be stopped," Raven stated matter-of-factly. Johni nodded.

"We need to get this stuff to the police."

"No," Raven said calmly, "we have to stop her ourselves."

"Excuse me?" Johni asked her eyes wide in astonishment. Raven turned to her and took Johni's hand in hers.

"If we don't stop her, she'll kill us both. The police are slow and they don't even believe it's her. She's not going to stop." Johni had to agree. Andi was a lunatic and convincing the police might take time they didn't have.

"Okay, you're right. What now?" Johni asked. As Raven was thinking the phone rang. They looked at each other and then Raven answered it.

"Yes?" She said into the receiver.

"Hi Raven." It was Andi.

"Hi Andi, what's up?" Raven asked looking into

Johni's eyes. Johni got down on her knees in front of Raven.

"Nothing, did you get my message?" Andi asked casually.

"Yes."

"How about we meet somewhere to discuss this break-up thing," Andi asked. "It could save the dykes life you know. Us gettin back together and all." Raven spoke carefully.

"If I do that will you leave Johni alone?"

"Sure I will," Andi answered sarcastically. Raven knew she was lying.

"Where then?" Raven asked.

"How bout KAT'S?" Andi asked, "Nice and public."

"Okay, what time?" It was turning her stomach to talk to Andi.

"Nine?"

"Nine is fine," Raven answered.

"Okie-doky," Andi sung, "see you then." Raven hung up the phone. She didn't have to explain anything about the conversation to Johni. She just joined her on her knees and held on to her for dear life.

* * *

Andi didn't know what made her decide all this now. She only knew that she had to even things up with Raven.

Sometimes ideas just came to her, like that time with that two year old and the curling iron. Oh hell, she thought, ain't got time for all that now. She had stuff to do. She didn't want Raven back she hated her. Besides she had actually FUCKED that dyke. She was unclean now. Andi smiled as she put on her clothes. She might not make it back tonight but she'd go out with a bang, of that she was certain, but she wasn't going out alone.

* * *

The Kat was crowded. Being here only served to remind Raven why she didn't come here anymore. From the look on Johni's face she was drawing the same conclusion. As if she had read her mind, Johni yelled to Raven over the music.

"This is exactly why I don't come to these places." Raven nodded. She lead Johni along the wall. She didn't want to chance Andi seeing them if she were already here. They made their way to the darkest corner of the club and began scanning the room for Andi. Raven had shown Johni a picture to refresh her memory of what Andi looked like. She didn't want any surprises. The music was good tonight. Briefly Raven wished they were there to enjoy themselves instead of to meet with Andi. She loved slow dancing with Johni and she was willing to bet that she was just as good a fast dancer. She re-focused her attentions on the dance floor. So far there was no sign of Andi. Raven reached over and grabbed Johni's hand. Johni squeezed it. Raven was about to tell her how she was feeling when a beautiful black woman appeared out of the crowd and approached Johni. Raven was instantly on her guard. The woman, a little taller than Raven, was very dark. She had an almost exotic look about her. She approached Johni and spoke.

"Hi," the woman said giving Johni a sexy look.

"Hello," Johni responded and resumed looking out into the crowd. Good, Raven thought passed the first test. The woman was not to be put off so easily. She put a hand on Johni's shoulder and whispered something in her ear. Raven was starting to seethe.

"No thank you, I'm with my girlfriend." Johni said over the music. Okay, Raven thought passed the second test. Raven moved closer to Johni who indicated her with a nod of her head to the woman. The woman disregarded Raven and reached up to put a hand in Johni's hair.

"I don't think so!" Raven yelled over the music, grabbing the woman's hand. The woman pulled her hand back and turned to confront Raven. Johni put a hand on the woman's arm.

"Why don't you take this somewhere else," Johni said sternly. The woman glared at Raven as the music died down. Finally she turned back to Johni.

"She will never be able to do for you what I can," The woman said quietly.

"Honcy, she already has," Johni said politely. Raven grinned from ear to ear. Johni passed this little test with flying colors. She grabbed Johni's arm and squeezed it tight. Johni looked over and smiled at Raven. Raven felt so blessed and protected. The music picked up and they continued their search. Johni and Raven stood in one spot looking for Andi for over an hour. Raven's feet were getting tired and Johni was getting impatient.

"Are you sure she will come?" Johni asked above the music.

"No, I'm not sure but I'd be willing to bet on it," Raven answered. Just as she was about to tell Johni that Andi was a determined person, Andi walked in the door.

"There she is," Raven whispered to Johni indicating the direction Andi was in. Raven took stock of Andi. She looked okay in fact she was smiling. She was carrying a sack in one hand. A woman was at her side, someone Raven didn't recognize.

"Who's that with her?" Johni asked.

"I don't know," Raven answered. They watched as Andi and her companion walked through the dance floor towards the bar. Raven had this sick feeling in her stomach just looking at Andi. She started forward but Johni pulled her back.

"What?" Raven said annoyance seeping into her voice.

"Let's do this right," Johni said quietly. "We need to confront her on our terms. Any ideas?" Raven thought for a moment and then an idea occurred to her.

"Let's just walk up to her," Raven answered. "What's she going to do in the middle of the dance floor? Hell, she won't know what to do." Johni considered for a moment. Andi could be dangerous even in here. She was still considering when out of nowhere Andi appeared.

"Hi," Andi said once they noticed her. She had gone up to the bar and ordered a drink. She handed it to Raven, who promptly sat it down on a table behind her.

"Hi yourself," Johni said sizing Andi up. Johni felt her stomach turn slightly.

"Jumpin place tonight." Andi said carefully. "It's always like this." Andi relocated to be next to Johni.

"What do you want?" Johni asked

"Your dick and her head," Andi replied haphazardly. Johni looked around to see if anyone else was listening to their conversation. If anyone was they weren't paying it any mind.

"That may be a little difficult," Johni said calmly. Andi smiled. Johni was about to say something else but before she could Raven pushed passed her.

"What do you want Andi?" Raven shouted. Andi looked at Raven and then back to Johni. The look in her eyes made Raven uncomfortable.

"I told you," Andi said smiling. The music seemed to become louder as they stood there. It was making Raven uncomfortable. She could barely hear Andi.

"Andi, things don't have to be this way," Raven said loudly. Andi laughed.

"Yes they do Raven. You started this mess. I was happy with you and you blew it." Andi stepped forward and Johni stepped in her path. Andi stepped back again and started laughing.

"Protecting her, Andrews?" Andi asked seemingly amused. "You couldn't protect a dog in a kennel let alone a woman. How ya feeling these days Andrews?" Johni was losing her patience. There were too many people in here; she had to get her outside. She took her best shot.

"The music's loud Andi, why don't we go outside," Johni shouted. Andi laughed yet again. The woman who had come in her appeared at her side again. Andi leaned back and kissed the woman long and hard. When she finished she looked at Raven and smiled.

"See Raven, you're not the only one who can get a whore." Raven started forward and Andi put out a hand.

"No you don't, Miss Thing." Andi bellowed, "You stay where you are." Raven was caught off guard by the anger in Andi's voice. For the first time Raven wondered if they should have just called the police. Andi smiled.

"You underestimate me Raven. I have nothing to lose," Andi said carefully, "When you have nothing to lose you tend to not care anymore what happens to you. If your girlfriend here hadn't had that iron-clad stomach, she'd already be dead. It's amazing what a little rat poisoning can do when mixed in antibiotics." Realizing what she was suggesting Johni and Raven both started forward. Andi stepped back and put an arm around the woman she'd come with her. From behind the woman's back Andi produced a knife. Before either Johni or Raven could react Andi plunged the knife into the woman's back. Raven screamed and for the first time people around them realized something was wrong. The music played on as the woman Andi stabbed sank to the floor. Somewhere someone else screamed. Raven felt sick to her stomach. Andi stood staring at her holding the blood-drenched knife up for Raven to see.

"You see, Raven, I have nothing to lose now," Andi offered, "With you I didn't kill anymore but since you no longer want me I have no choice."

The look in Andi's eyes was frightening. Raven reached back for Johni who took her hand. Andi watched the exchange and laughed even harder. A clearing was opening around them now. Suddenly the music stopped. All eyes became focused on the three of them.

"You think she's going to save you, Raven?" What a

joke. She can't save you. She can't save anyone." She's rambling, Raven thought. Beside her Johni tensed. Andi waved the sack she had in her hand in Raven's face. "She can't save anyone. I can proved it!" Andi took a step back and addressed the crowd. "She can't help anyone. I have someone who can attest to that!" Andi turned to Johni. "She called out for you, Johni. She also told me that you were a good fuck! But you know what, I was a better fuck. I FUCKED HER TO DEATH!" Andi opened the sack and dumped the contents out on the floor. Brenda's severed head fell to the floor with a sickening thud and rolled to Johni and Raven's feet. As people realized what it was they panicked and started to run towards the doors. Raven grabbed Johni who was staring, horrified at the head at her feet.

"Oh, my God Raven," Johni breathed, "it's Brenda. The body belonged to Brenda." Johni sounded detached and far away. Raven didn't look down. She knew if she did she'd lose it. She looked into Johni's eyes and realized she was in shock. Her stomach heaved and for a couple of moments she felt her own sanity waning. Without a second thought Raven lunged at Andi. Andi hadn't been expecting the move and it caught her off guard. Raven knocked Andi to the floor. She landed with a thud, Raven on top of her. Andi recovered quickly however and scrambled to her feet. Raven hopped up and readied herself.

"Good, Raven," Andi said breathing hard. "Good move caught me off guard." Andi lunged at Raven but Raven's size allowed her to duck the blow. Andi found herself facing the wrong direction. She turned quickly and faced Raven again. Raven stole a glance at Johni who was just now realizing what was going on. Raven quickly turned her attention back to Andi. She couldn't worry about Johni right now. Andi had the knife in her hand and Raven realized that if she weren't careful she'd end up on the wrong end of that blade. Andi hesitated. Raven saw something change slightly in her face. She took a chance.

"Andi, let me help you," Raven pleaded.

"Help me?" Andi asked, "Help me what?" She laughed loudly.

"You're sick, Andi, and there are people who can help," Raven offered, "Just put the knife down and let me help." Andi seemed to consider for a moment.

"Will you come back to me?" She asked in a small voice. Raven recognized that voice. Andi used it every time she was insecure.

"Yes, Andi, I'll come back. You just need to get better first," Raven eased. Out of the corner of her eye, she noticed Johni moving. From the look in Johni's eyes she had come out of her shock. "Let's call the police together. We can get this whole thing straightened out," Raven assured her. Raven hoped that she was sounding convincing.

Andi suddenly turned pale. Raven was sure that Andi was about to hit the floor.

"Raven please," Andi pleaded. Raven just turned and indicated that Andi should follow her and she did. Johni was perplexed but she followed as well. Although Andi still had the knife in her hand she was behind Raven like a small child. They went outside to where Raven's car was parked. Andi leaned against the car.

"Get off my car," Raven said sternly. Andi jumped up as if the car had burned her.

"I didn't mean to hurt anyone," Andi started.

"Do you think that excuses what you did?" Raven reprimanded. "You killed people." Andi started to cry. Raven motioned for Johni to step closer.

"It was your fault!" Andi screamed. Raven wanted to slap her but instead she played along. She had to keep her calm until the police arrived. Raven didn't want anyone else hurt.

"My fault? How was it my fault?!" Raven asked.

"I followed you! You left and I knew that you weren't going where you said you were! I followed you and I saw where you went! I knew you were meeting someone!" Andi screamed through her tears. Raven could say nothing at this point, she knew that Andi would just have to get it out. She hoped to waste time until the police arrived. A small crowd had begun to build back off in the darkness. People were watching to see what was going to happen next. Part of Raven was embarrassed that she was a part of this scene, but also relieved by the crowd. Andi seemed to be losing it, at least this way she had witnesses.

"I knew what you were up to!" Andi continued. "I figured you were seeing some bitch! I never dreamed it would be a writer! What's wrong Raven this little store clerk was not good enough for you?!" Andi turned to Johni and Johni readied herself. She didn't know what Andi might do next. She was hysterical. "All she wants is your money! She's greedy and selfish! She won't care about your feelings. She'll tell you that you're stupid and crazy! She'll keep you from your family!" Andi collapsed to the ground breathing hard and crying. Raven felt a distant need to help her but that was quickly squelched with Andi's next line. "She doesn't even like sex! She uses it to keep you in line. If you're good she'll give it up! Isn't that right Raven?!"

Raven had heard enough. She quickly closed the two steps between herself and Andi and slapped Andi hard across the face. Andi lunged forward at Raven, knife in hand. Raven hit her again, much harder. Andi fell to the ground. She stayed there for a minute and then Raven heard a growling much like an animal about to charge. She realized, at the last moment, it was coming from Andi.

Andi got to her feet and jumped at Raven again. This time Johni caught Andi in mid-air. Raven watched in horror as the blade of Andi's knife buried itself in Johni's shoulder.

"Johni!" Raven cried. Johni wretched away from Andi and shoved her backward. The knife was still embedded in her shoulder.

"You don't think I can protect a woman you crazy bitch?!" Johni yelled. "Then come on!

"Andi came at Johni and, in one simple move, Johni stepped to the side seizing Andi around the chest. She reached up with her bad hand and tore the knife from her shoulder. In seconds she had the knife at Andi's throat. Andi tried, half-heartedly, to pull free but realized that Johni was in a better position than she was.

"I believe you want to think about that real hard before you make that decision," Johni stated calmly. Andi stopped struggling. She started crying again. Johni had to fight the urge to slit her throat, in the distance sirens wailed.

"Let me go!" Andi whined. "I couldn't have done anything to stop it, he made me do it." She was rambling but Johni didn't loosen her grip. She didn't trust her. Andi tried to drop to the ground but Johni just tighten her hold. "She did it. Don't you see, Andi cried pointing at Raven, she made me mad. She hurt me. That's why I did it. It was her fault." It was obvious that Andi was not going to take any blame for this. Johni looked back at Raven.

"Are you okay?" She asked her. Raven nodded her head, she was crying.

"Look at her cry!" Andi screamed. "I'll kill you bitch, you'll never be able to sleep again," she screamed at Raven, "I'm going to be your nightmare!" Johni tightened her grip. Two black and whites pulled into the club parking lot. Several policemen jumped out, guns drawn. Detective Collins, the detective from the hospital interview, emerged from the second car.

The owner of the Kat came out when the police arrived. She had seen the entire thing and explained it to the officers. One of the officers handcuffed Andi. Raven ran to Johni and put her arm around her. Johni was bleeding badly. They walked over to the police cruiser and Johni leaned against the car.

"No!" Andi screamed. "You can't arrest me! Arrest her!" She pointed at Raven. "It's her fault! Arrest her!" The officers put Andi into the back seat of the police car. She continued to scream. Collins approached Johni and Raven.

"We'll need you both to come down to the station tomorrow for statements." They both nodded. "We put out an arrest warrant on Miss. Lancaster earlier today. We received a call from a local hotel she was staying in. There's a headless corpse in the room she was renting.

Johni and Raven remained silent. There simply wasn't anything else to say.

"Thank you officer," Johni said. We'll be down in the morning."

"You'd better get to a doctor about that shoulder," Collin suggested. Johni nodded.

When the police car Andi was in pulled off, she was still screaming in the back seat. Raven shook her head.

"I never knew," she said softly.

"Come on, let's go Raven," Johni urged quietly. As the crowd dissipated Johni and Raven got into the MG.

"I guess we'd better go to the hospital first," Johni suggested. Raven leaned over and hugged Johni gently.

"Does it hurt badly?" She asked. Johni smiled.

"I think we did okay, considering."

"I love you Johni," Raven said rubbing Johni's arm. Johni leaned over and kissed Raven's nose.

"I love you too, Raven. We're going to be okay," she reassured. Raven put the car in gear and pulled out of the parking lot. Neither of them noticed the woman in the dark blue sedan across the street. Inside the car the woman was rocking back and forth stroking the hair of a doll.

"It's okay, they won't get away with it," she said stroking the doll's head harder. "Nobody treats my little girl like that and gets away with it." The voice inside her head boomed. "Make them pay, mother, or you'll have to answer to ME!" William Lancaster was a frightening man, even dead.

"I'll take care of it," Ida Lancaster told her husband.

"If you don't you know what'll happen don't you?"

"Yes."

"What'll happen, mother?" The voice mocked.

"You'll make me suffer," she said quietly. William Lancaster's laughter filled the car. Lightly kissing the doll on the forehead, Mrs. Lancaster put the doll down and started the car. "I'll take care of it, William," she whispered as tears welled up in her eyes. "I'll make them pay."

Acknowledgements

Many thanks to those who made this book possible. To my kids, Aaron, Ryan, Jordan and Jessa, for the countless "hang on a minutes" they endured. To my better half, TyAnne, who read every word and was honest about it even when I didn't want her to be.

To my publisher Re.ad Publishing, Inc. for giving Passion's Revenge a home. A special thanks to Amanda Barnett of Re.ad Publishing for nursing me through the process.

To my readers and fans…Johni and Raven wouldn't have a life if it weren't for you all.